VIOLE
SOLUTIONS
TO
POPULAR
PROBLEMS

Stories

M.J. NICHOLLS

Sagging
Meniscus

Set in Williams Caslon Text with LATEX.

ISBN: 978-1-952386-53-4 (paperback)
ISBN: 978-1-952386-62-6 (ebook)
Library of Congress Control Number: 2023937318

Sagging Meniscus Press
Montclair, New Jersey
saggingmeniscus.com

In memory of
Royce M. Becker
A catherine wheel of creative pizzazz

&

Brian Hamill
A fallen crusader for fine literature

Contents

VIOLENT SOLUTIONS

to Popular Problems

Librarian of the Year

A S THE CARROTY cinderblock of the X99 approached, Isobel mused on the moment in history busses passed from hip to square to retro. The classic currant-coloured Thurso bus—that exquisitely uncomfortable Brum-faced icebox, careening at speed along the Highland coast— was now viewed as an aesthetic triumph, a comical tribute to the cheery weariness of the far-removed ruddy-faced Nanooks of the north. A testament to the stoicism of the people, content to risk shivering in a rattly coffin one ill-timed swerve away from a cinematic North Sea kiss. Stepping into the toasty Stagecoach, swiftly bagging the leg-stretcher by the fire exit door, cracking open Octave Mirbeau's *Le Calvaire*, she concluded modern transport was preferable to being stranded at 8.30PM in Ulbster catching sleet in your teeth.

"That's offensive," a mouth said.

"Pardon?" Isobel asked, identifying the mouth-owner as the opposite seat occupant.

"Your mask."

Isobel's choice of virus containment was a black mask with the caption 'Read Books, You C**ts', a cloth personally woven for her by Betty Straithmore, a teenager who'd knitted her way through 1,281 YouTubes.

"The trend for motivational swearing is one that has passed you by?" she asked.

"There are kids on this bus," the woman with the leathery skin of Iggy Pop and the steam-ironed tresses of Iggy Pop said.

"There are two lessons woven into this four-word provoke," Isobel explained. "The first lesson concerns the importance of reading or— to magic up a more satisfying phrasal boom-bang-a-lang—squirting the salvation of literary cream between the filo pastry of human despair. The second lesson concerns the reclamation of the so-called swear as an agency of pep, to propel people from their slouch toward better ways of thinking and understanding, rather than relying on the words as lazy verbal slaps to insult and debase others. As a concession to the weasily offended, the knitter, you will observe, has censored the word, and yet you still appear pouty."

"I think it's wrong."

"Down on the street, the faces shine when they see my mask. You must have a real low mind. You'd rather I removed?"

"You have to wear a face-covering at all times."

"In which case, have a pleasant ride, and while you're at it, read a book you quidnunc cunt."

This last causing Iggy to move twelve seats forward.

2

On returning to the topological crumbs of Orkney, a place that swatted away lunacy with the efficiency of a lizard slurping a winged termite in temporary respite on a crag, from a loft in London Soho that she'd rented with royalties from the works of recently self-ended critic Raine Upright, Isobel perused the mail at her ex-ex-cottage home to note she had won Librarian of the Year 2020, sponsored by Oxo Stock Cubes. The ceremony was located at The Savoy hotel—a hop-skip-and-a-bound from her previous address—where she was required to receive the trophy from Liam Neeson in four days.

This news was a solid unction on her severely scorched chi. Her occupation of the Soho loft with serially bland hack-writer-cum-reader-of-one-thousand books and temporary protagonist of the fêted *The 1002nd Book to Read Before You Die* Marcus Schott had been a time of heavyweight territorial pissing. His writerly insecurity and feverish attempts to emporken the slip of literary talent he possessed by pounding on the sandalwood planks spluttering out criminally poor plotlines ("Man stalks a man who turns out to be the very man he has been stalking!") and cringey one-liners for insertion into the mouths of his cardboard antiheroes ("Why, that's a marvellously *astringent* retort, my half-Belgian friend!") had been tiresome.

She had learned that writers, removed from the snuggly novelty of hour-long pop-ins at libraries and workshops, were irritating and unlikeable 87% of the time. At a brie-and-beer *sindig* (as titled) to celebrate an unpublished fax by Anaïs Nin, the novelist Adam Mars-Jones cornered her with a lecture on the youth's "militant" wielding of the pilcrow. The patchy noughties-known Adam Thirlwell lamented no-one had remarked how *Lurid & Cute*, his extremely annoying blabber of a last novel, had been an allegory for the purposelessness of post-Castro Cuba. Isobel missed her status as she-Goddess of the Orkney Library where she had transformed the populace from a subliterate mess of rustics fondling ewes in sheepcotes to rustics who could recite portions of *Buddenbrooks* while fondling ewes in sheepcotes.

3

As Isobel ceased her awkward crouching over the WC, keeping both cheeks twelve inches away from the rim while averting minor head trauma on the sink courtesy of the bus's jounce, she eared a slow bleating lowing from a backrow. The slow-bleater in a backrow was a young woman aping a Jean Seberg *Breathless*-bob, clad in a lemony cagoule, her weepy head hung over the 1995 Dalkey Archive edition of Rikki Ducornet's *The Stain*. Unkeen to involve herself in another's soapy palaver, the presence of Rikki wowed Isobel near.

"There's nothing like the sumptuous Carrollian surrealism of Lady Duc on a pissy Tuesday," she said as an opener, kneeling on the seat before Seberg.

"What?"

"I'm assuming you're too weepy to natter on the matter. Whyforth the weeps?"

"It's nothing."

"Lordy, lady. You'd have me blindly fumble your innermosts to prise the reason from you with my callipers of curiosity?"

"It's my girlfriend. She's made off with my manuscript."

"Expand."

"I was back with my parents in Wick scooping up thingies from my room to take to my new flat in Edinburgh. Hairbands, Stereo Total vinyl, Henrik Tjele erotica . . . that sort of thingie. Another was the novel I wrote on a vintage Underwood I was intending to submit to publishers. When I returned, I found a note in place of the manuscript that said 'LITERARY FAME OR SEXY DAME? Come to me.' On the note was an address in Brora. That's where I'm . . ."

"Heading?"

"Yes."

"And the tears?"

"I'd been writing the novel for five years. It was supposed to be my audacious literary entrée. We were on the cusp of breaking up, so I'm worried she's destroyed the novel in some creatively twisted way for extra hurt."

Isobel, noting how her kneeling-with-elbows-propped-casually-over-the-seat-in-front position clashed with the whiny tone, sat next to Seberg and patted the arms of her cagoule, making the supportive sound of creased nylon.

"Stealing someone's unpublished novel is among the most criminally low act of lowly criminality ever conceived. Your lover is a louse, Unnamed Woman. I tell you, I've seen some cutthroat revenge attempts in my time, but that takes the entire cake factory. Raine Upright once concreted every hole in a golf course when the owner snubbed him at a kiosk. That was morally special revenge. Another time, he spiked the beer of a local racist, then applied brown body paint to his entire skin to teach him a lesson about not being a bigoted twonk. When he lived in Wigan, he was spiking people hourly. What can her motive be?"

"She's trying to wound me."

"Nah."

"Sorry?"

"You wouldn't abscond with someone's opus to cause temporary nips. There's a nifty psychological play here, or is there?"

"I don't know."

"Let me help you."

4

The weeper was Clara Draywort, current resident of Wick who had spurned the common path of a securely shrinkwrapped bourgeois nipper—from scenically positioned childhood idyll-home to Big Town, pockets heaving with a parental stipend—but had remained in the royal borough to hone her nous as a novelist.

She calculated that by cultivating an unusual history for herself, her chances of market success were seriously bumped. A queer and totally-alt freakozoid from a backwater pastiching a lass in a Belle & Sebastian song had more commercial cachet than the sullen child of two arch Scottish Tories who read mainly Robert Harris. She chose to reinvent herself before she had invented herself, a process she called "pre-inversion", building herself a new self by swapping all her least desirable traits with their polar opposites.

She replaced her fondness for Stravinsky with fondness for Sleaford Mods and The Wedding Present. She flipped her sexuality. She preferred the scope (and hipness) being queer offered in the hyper-liberal literary world, even though she was pretty sure of her heterosexuality, having frequently creamed to Google images of Kit Harington. This is where Petra Shrike made her appearance. A local polystyrene heiress, only sprog of the thermoplastics innovator Oliver Shrike, she first made herself known to Clara in a copse, wearing only her pants and a cardboard mask of cyberpunk writer Kathy Acker.

Lust and obsession came next.

Isobel and Clara shed the bus in Brora, ugging along the seafront paying no attention to the scenically identikit views.

"We're not about to uncover Petra lying with her wrists slit, are we?" Isobel asked as they approached a shabby holiday cottage plopped on a hillock.

"Her daddy probably owns this," Clara said.

"You never answered me."

"Petra's not the wrist-slitting type. She'd want her suicide to be an artistic bonanza like some feminist rebuke of David Bowie's *Blackstar*. She once talked about having herself taxidermied in the very act of expiration."

"Getting stuffed in real time."

"Exactly."

"Cool lady."

They approached the cottage's plasterbored off-cream frontage, peering in the window at the sort of chair usually occupied by an expiring oldster staring numbly at death's moody horizons. The front door was open. On the kitchen table was the first page of Clara's novel alongside an address in Golspie, a town six miles south.

"She's leading you to her, page by page," Isobel said.

Clara stood reading her opener, checking for any retributive desecration of her manuscript. Satisfied that everything was in place, she folded the page for insertion in her handbag.

"Can I have look?" Isobel asked.

"If it's okay, I'd rather not, I hate sharing work in progress."

"Hmm. Sure."

Uh-ohs exploded in Isobel's mind.

"I appreciate you coming with me, Isobel, but I can't expect you to stay, if this is to be a long, tedious trip."

"We'll see. For now, onward to Golspie!"

5

The short bus trip to Golspie—when the rare sighting of a bus occurred— yielded another empty cottage and the second page of

Clara's manuscript. She received the page with the same scrutiny, squinting intently at her own lines like an art dealer on the scent of forgery, and concealed the page cagily again in her handbag. This secretiveness activated literary flashbulbs in Isobel's head.

In her formidable run-up to becoming Britain's most lauded librarian, she had impeccable insight into the perennial quirks of poets and novelists. All the authors she had encountered were desperate to foist their prose on absolutely anyone, running up to you with the sugary zest of a toddler eager to share their drawing of a fat sheep with the world. Some transgress social expectations to capture the eyes of a receptive reader. After a reading in Orkney, Alan Warner once waited two hours in the rain for the library to close, then sprang from a shrub with the opening line of his new one *Gloopier Than Thou*, shuddering in anticipation of Isobel's warm reception. Jonathan Lethem sought her take on his hourly rewrites one summer, bombarding her inbox with updates, creatively paralysed without a kindly word of response. Jonathan Littell once offered her £50,000 to be his "in-house" soundboard, to literally camp in his apartment and respond to his every completed sentence across the entire composition of his novel. This being the case, there was something suspicious about the coy ones.

She recalled the time Bo Fowler leapt across the room to prevent her taking a peep at printouts of his newest story. Later, she read the appalling tale in print. It was a sloppy, bland squib on parenthood, the sort of runny yolk usually seen in the Reader's Digest. Then there was Jane Rogers, author of *The Ice is Singing*, whose whiffy memoir was leaked to Isobel by her worried husband, clearly identifying a turkey in the first line: *Ring ring! Wakey-wakey, let the day coagulate!* Then there was Alison Lurie, who famously clutched a manuscript so tightly to her bosom, her publisher had to butter his hands to free the egregiously composed pages from her deathly clench. It was clear to Isobel she'd been wrong to trust this young woman.

Her mission had volte-faced in her face. Rather than valiantly rushing to the aid of this victim of theft by a cowardly louse of a lover who had snatched her work away in a pathetic act of revenge, she wondered whether this Petra was exposing her lover to this ordeal for a nobler aim. To convince Clara that her lover was more important than her manuscript, to invest her energies in the romance as a way of signalling that her talent was either nonexistent or that her opinion of her contrived self was overly inflated.

Either way, Isobel had to sample the prose immediately.

6

On sparsely occupied buses, where the two sat tight-lipped in contemplation of their conflicting objectives, the trip moved south to Tain and Dingwall, bypassing Inverness, along the Moray coast to Forres, Cullen, Peterhead, and Stonehaven. When they arrived at the charming town of Montrose, sitting for a spot of tea by the fire in a B&B, Isobel seized the moment to pinch a page from Clara's handbag when she went to the bathroom. When Clara returned, she excused herself to read the opener on the toilet.

The clearly perceived spider crept along Muriel's cornice. The night was approaching with the heaving doom of a midnight rapist.

"Fuck me," Isobel said.

"She must be stopped," she said next.

Over a plate of exquisite salmon, Isobel smiled weakly, barely masking her freshly whisked, lip-wibbling contempt. Clara had morphed from a sweet, mixed-up lass to a contemptible cretin with no redeeming qualities whatsoever in a mere two sentences.

"Are you OK?" Clara asked.

"I'm peachy, sweetie," she said.

The next day, following an overnight stay, Isobel detoured to Dundee, where she printed the pdf instruction manual for a Shark Anti-Hair Wrap Cordless Vacuum Cleaner from her email at the Central Library. Her plan was to swap the pages in Clara's handbag with the printed ones, then brutally incinerate her originals to shield the world from such criminal sentences.

Creeping further down the coast, with stops in Crail, Leven, and Aberdour, the twenty completed pages were recovered, and Clara was reunited with Petra in the Meadows, Edinburgh, where her thieving lover sat Indian-style with her palms proffered in a vaguely pretentious way, attempting to counter any oncoming fume with a Zen-like display of loving receptivity.

"This is where I leave you," Isobel said.

"Thank you so much for helping me," Clara said.

"Uh-huh."

She swerved the hug by pleading lateness for her train. Only six hours remained to zip to London for her award.

7

Two weeks' later, Isobel received a letter from Petra:

Dear Isobel,

When you appeared alongside Clara that afternoon in the Meadows, I had taken you for a meddling aunt come to administer stern thwacks of disciplinary sass to my cheeks. Clara explained that you were a librarian she had bumped into on the bus, and that you had volunteered your services at tracking down the pages of the manuscript I had placed in my parents' various rental properties along the eastern coast. My intention was that upon making the trip, Clara would learn a form of introspection formerly lacking in the twee maiden persona she had cultivated for herself and shake her real self free from this oppressive persona to reveal the honest person she was underneath, and all that cheesy malarky, the person I had been trying for so long to convince her was worthy of her consideration.

I also fervently hoped that she came to realise that her obsessive pursuit of literary plaudits was not commensurate with her actual talents, and several evenings in draughty seaside rentals alone might force her to reread her work in a new light. You can understand my annoyance when I heard that you had not only accelerated her trip to meet your own schedule, almost catching me up, and that you had taken her side against what you perceived was a heinous affront to a potentially scintillant new voice in literature. (Yes, I am suppressing a snigger).

As soon as you quit the scene, Clara flipped her infernal wig at me, screaming "you're a traitress to art" repeatedly, and that my actions were unforgivable, and that I should rot in hell, etc. I was reduced to begging her to hear my version of events, and managed to weepily strongarm her to a café, where it was revealed that you had replaced the pages of her manuscript with those of a vacuum cleaner manual.

It occurred to me immediately that you had read samples of Clara's work and came to the same conclusion as me—that to release this torrentially weak prose into the hands of any unsuspecting reader was a crime against literature, and that she simply must be stopped.

Her reaction to this news was one of yelping incredulity. She ran back to the Meadows stomping her rainbow-stickered crocs as if crushing the critics beneath her feet, raving to me about reporting you to the police, having you murdered, or tailing you to London and exposing you as manipulative liar at your awards ceremony. I managed to sedate her with softly-cadenced phonemes and take her to my flat.

There, I explained that the destruction of her work was a necessary character unblocker, a way for her to realise her selfhood as a fairly drab character from Wick who should probably pursue a career in property law with me.

She affirmed my correctness, and we're currently studying property law at St. Andrew's, although sadly she's shed her queerness, and we no longer constitute an item.

Yours,

Petra Shrike

8

In her speech at The Savoy to the assembled, Isobel said:

"It's not merely the role of the librarian to politely prod readers in the direction of soul-twirling reads that will forever fire their imaginations, to maintain an ordered and unmolested stock, or to shock snoozing elders awake by poking them with a broom handle. It's also our civic responsibility to convince aspirant writers to pursue other artistic ambitions. It's imperative, in an age when *Twilight* fan fiction plagues the bestseller shelves, that we recognise the atrociously untalented and stop them from polluting our libraries with their dire outpourings. In my time, I have identified hundreds of pushy non-talents who spend their days thrusting themselves forward and talking up the magnificence of their book ideas before a single word has been written. For these shysters, the prose itself is secondary to the hype around the work itself, what we call the *epitext*.

"I would like to further illustrate this point by referring to a letter I received from novelist Zacharia Hoss, who wrote to me on the pre-launch palpitations ahead of an event for his 'post-orbital ravioli western' *Dead Liquor Store*.

"I explained to Zacharia that the act of authoring is a mysterious process—a hyper-holy consecration between the imagination and the page. As an author, you must protect this unknowable, super-sacred sanctitic process, and the shimmering halos of heavenly prose you sweat from your imperial pores.

"If you've ever slobbered your way through several yonks of literary studies, you may have heard of French notioneer Gérard Genette's coinage *paratext*—a termic pater for texts orbiting the text itself, spawning the children *peritext* (titles, notes, prefaces) and *epitext* (blurbs, reviews, interviews). Genette labels these paratexts "a zone between text and off-text [. . .] at the service of a better reception of the text." I would like to, if you will permit me, heave Genette's scruffy theory out to sea on a schooner of contempt.

"The epitext is your enemy, I explained. Everything in the epitextual realm seeks to undermine the potency of that unknowable process of authoring I mentioned mere minims ago by forcing the wibbling bag of frailty and chin-stroking responsible for the novel (you) into sparsely occupied rooms where you are invited to piss upon this process by publicly mangling your words, turning the focus away from the merits of their magic to the humiliating reality of your bodily flumps—your stammer, your accent, your hideousness—anything to skew the viewer to the prospect that your prose probably resembles this inadequate self. Or, that sentence in shorter form, they will equate your many bodily bloopers with the calibre of your prose. The two have no connection, I said, using as an example my own author M.J. Nicholls.

"His first book (the offensively under-reviewed dystopian literary satire *The House of Writers*) was "launched" (I have serious qualms with this verb, but that's for next year's speech—wink wink) in 2016 in a vegan caff frequented by quondam humanities students and molesters of earnestness unwowed in the presence of high literary voltage—everyday Facebook selfists who love nibbling vegan kibble in the vicinity of high literary voltage while completely shunning the reading, the author, and the book—swatting away any offers of taking a cursory glance at the printed object itself—while blathering about their upcoming retreats to corporate internships as they end their artistic phase and enter their lifespans reading one book a year.

"To avoid the embarrassment of speaking his words in a hesitant and shaky manner to roomful of indifferent falafel-munchers, Nicholls hired a voice actor to read selected slices of illustratively twinkly prose, and plopped himself in tatty chair to sip prosecco and chuckle heartily to himself at his own risibility. He was back in his teenage bedroom, making himself chuckle to pass the lonely Sunday mornings with violent cartoons and forays into comic listicles before listicles were a thing. Here, at the apex of his literary ambitions, he sat semi-drunk in a chair, watching a paid actor read his own prose back to him, entirely for his own amusement. This reaffirmed his view that the writer writes for his or herself, and any audience for their work is utterly accidental. In that particular room, the book he wrote for his own amusement was being launched entirely for his own amusement for the intended audience of one—him—and as much as his invited friends surrendered smirks of solidarity at the notion of him ever trying his hand at "public authorship"— there was no denying the Onan of this -ism.

"So, I concluded to Zacharia, for me, there is no higher reward for the prose writer than the way the prose the prose writer has written pirouettes across the prosey prose-face of their prosily prosèd pages. The only pleasure in authorship resides in that collision of word upon word, the surf of syllables ten-fiving across the page with the fleet boardwork of a seasoned sea-dude, and the magisterial power in corralling the imagination into utterly sublime sentences of epic sensuality . . . possessing a temporary form of mastery over something in a world utterly untameable and unlovable.

"Turning up to literary events, surrounded by your well-intentioned, envious, or embarrassed peers, less than 1% of whom may end up actually reading (some) of your words, is nothing less than a ritual humiliation for an author. If you wish to despoil your creations, I explained, if you wish to subject your little ripples of lexical magic to acres of hurt, the worst thing you can do is to show yourself in public and feed your brilliance to the ravenous vampires of epitext. The text has its place on the page and must remain there.

"But to return to my central point. It is incumbent on the librarian to spot no-talent and squish hard before they run amok in our world. I recently had the opportunity of destroying the first novel of an ambitious young poseur and expect to receive a warm letter of thanks for my efforts. When you enter your library and see shelves of slurry buffered by brilliant literary beacons, you can rest assured that the librarians are responsible for maintaining those beacons and preventing an entire takeover of tripe from terrorising the nation.

"Not to toot our own trumpets, but librarians are the brave warriors presently preventing the entirety of western civilisation from crumpling into a drooly slump.

"It is to those unsung heroes, like me, that I dedicate my award.

"Thank you."

Heath's Ledger

IN OUR PELL-MELL, consumerist hellscape, the things designed to give us pleasure often cause us the most pain.

Take the billboard, par example. Stock-still in a honking morass of hatchbacks and motorhomes, we observe the actress Kate Winslet in a rare state of dress, peddling perfume with her slap-caked visage and strawberry tresses playfully blown athwart. The advert sells the promise of pleasure: the lure of romance or sexual congress through the nasal means of chemical chicanery. At the same time, the posed pout of this A-lister, using her status to swipe a minor fortune by featuring her face as we honk ourselves through clots of black smoke to rooms with clapboard, IKEA drawers, and twats, plants a bitter seed. We envy her beauty, wealth, power, and status. We resent the implication that our proletarian oxters require an overpriced squirt to make us soignée human beings. The outcome . . . pure pain.

Or, nibble on this. We fatten our hampers with lox and crepes for an afternoon in the marvellous Newport sunshine, but the 25° heat over-whelms our palish skin and we must scoff our edibles below Gregor's contiguous tarp. Or, these. The long-awaited blockbuster with Tim Hut-ton as a cockless spiv is a piece of overblown artistic limescale. The speed-sizzled £20 shrimp we ordered tastes like wet cardboard on two blancmanges. The foam bath with laurel-infused bubblage we ran has run colder than a cup of rime.

Etcetera.

In 2013, I began to ponder on the balance of pleasure versus pain. I calculated I was in pain, whether minor ouches or major aaarghs, 50% more than I was in snuggle-bedded warm-tootsied puh-puh-pleasure. I knew, in the words of The Stranglers from their seminal second LP, that something better change. First, I looked at the felicific calculus. This is an algorithm used to determine the amount of pleasure present in each separate action. There are seven vectors to this algorithm, which I will now illustrate.

Example. I am a peckish man. I wish to eat a cupcake from the fridge. The following must be taken into consideration:

How strong is the pleasure? *Salted-caramel-and-macchiato-icing-strong.*

How long will it last? *Until the cupcake has been licked, nibbled, and chomped clear.*

Is it probable pleasure will occur? *As sure as night follows night in Murmansk.*

How soon? *From lick one to lick final.*

Is it likely this action will be followed by similar sensations? *There are two cupcakes left, so yes.*

Is it likely this action will be followed by opposite sensations? *If the cupcake is left in the fridge, it will harden, creating an inedible loam of sugary detritus unfit for the lowliest serf.*

How many people will be affected? *One, though if my flatmate craved a cupcake in future, bigly sulks would abound for that unlucky cupcake expector denied her bliss.*

The algorithm was created as part of Benthamian utilitarianism to explore the moral outcomes for communities seeking to sop maximum happiness from the societal sponge, favour to be found in an upward vector of pleasure (*hedons*), and frowns in a downward (*dolors*). I concluded that a life of ethical hedonism was a non-starter, that the pleasure vectors would plummet with repetition, reducing previous pleasures to the same level of ho-hum as quotidian strifes and struggles. Instead, I sought to achieve a perfect balance between pleasure and pain. Using the felicific method to determine the validity of each pleasure or pain, I would add the relevant sensations to a simple ledger and attempt a perfect balance at the end of each day. If I found myself in pleasure credit, I would do something I disliked to restore equilibrium, and vice versa. An example from Day One:

Pleasure	Pain
Croissant and chai latte	Toe stubbed on kitchen table
Earwormed Shakira in the car	Stuck in traffic
Tittersome tale from colleague Tamara	Terminal printer swallowed Report 2(B)
Tetris—350 rows	Pie and mash *in extremis*
Mild rush hour traffic	Escalator snub from boss
Pie and mash *a Deo*	No chocolates left for pudding
Will Self on Channel 4 News	Poor Netflix doc on Chindits
Strident self-administered orgasm	No sleep until 1AM

You will observe, and perhaps scoff, at the inexact science of this, at the absence of exacting or concrete variables to perceive one item better or worse than the other, however, the intent was to establish a balance, not the pedantic quantification of each logged action in some ever-expanding database of activities. I omitted some of the smaller niggles—the wrigglework involved in ensuring chair comfort, the loud bang of an exhaust backfiring in the act of eating a banana, an overheard snatch of praise for Carmen Miranda, and so on. I practised this for a month, content knowing this balance was in place. This worked until, one afternoon, I met Ileana.

Ileana was transferred from the Cardiff branch of our pepper distribution outfit (we provided the United Kingdom with 69% of its peppercorns in sprinklable formats, until the hostile Nestlé takeover). Her brusque sentence structure, shorn clean of *ums*, *ahs*, *sos*, *hmms*, her penchant for pumping the quietest team members for notions, and her unapologetic blasting of *The Teaches of Peaches* in her office while writing reports on the optimum spice of a coarse corn were among her most striking qualities. She exuded the sentence: "The meteor flared red like a burning Icarus then exploded over Jupiter in a spectacular bulge of light." I prebooked a twelve-course tasting menu in readiness for a heft of pain in the event of a knockback, then asked her on a date. "Tomorrow @ 6, The Bitchin' Kitchen?" she replied.

Our first night together required careful balancing. I was so thrilled at the prospect of our public coupling I experienced no real pain all afternoon. Ileana served me furtive looks across the scanner, her smirk at a sizzling gradient of sauce. I bristled with anticipation and arousal. To redress the balance, I had to steal moments of unpleasantness whenever I could—knocking back out-of-date milk from the depths of the staff canteen fridge, scrubbing clean the office toilets, cancelling my virus protection software. I was exhausted when 6PM rolled around. I even considered causing a minor traffic accident to counter the bliss of anticipation. Instead, I imagined how our date might fail—our meal punctuated with awkward silences, clashing personalities, cheap plonk. I slapped on the aftershave, suited up, and poured myself into the street.

Ileana was seated when I arrived. Her meteoric red bob, hellraisered with a strategic paradox of hairpins, her slender frame sleeked into a purple top and black mini, her steel-rimmed spectacles sitting at a cool slouch upon her button nose, caused cartwheels of sensation in me, the sort that would require a six-week stretch in Wormwood Scrubs to create the illusion of restoring "balance". I affected a casual breeziness as she watched me cross the buffed parquet floor of this unbustling Moroccan-American restaurant.

"You're ten minutes early," she said. "I'm not one for that keep-the-man-waiting routine. Torturing someone from the off sets a bad precedent."

"That's humungous wisdom," I said.

"It is. So . . . looking forward to an evening of couscous, vodka chasers, and athletic sexual intercourse?"

"Whatsat?"

"You might think I'm making a remark to neutralise the tension or lobbing a flirt for fun while we await our kefta meatballs or smouldering shank of mechoui. But I'm serious. You *are* up for hours of athletic sexual intercourse afterwards, aren't you?" she asked.

"Yes, of course. It was the threat of couscous that made me hesitate," I said, hoping the waiter who arrived had not heard this flip dismissal of their national staple.

"In fact, let's skip dinner, shall we? Now that I've raised the agenda, neither of us will be able to concentrate. We should commence the rutting and summon a pizza after if we have the inclination."

"Good idea."

"I'm full of them."

We made our apologies to the waiter, hopped in a cab, and bedded down at her place.

She plunged at once into the wildness of my undershirt, strumming my shoulders, chest, and back like a stool-based concert pianist caressing the cadences of Herr Schubert. Her kisses were meta-kisses—kisses so consummate their kind had heretofore never been categorised in the world of kisses—kisses that seemed to encompass several kissing strata at once, from the cinematic smooch to the tongue-deep Frencher to the classic teenage lip-noshing. I was about to experience an avalanche of pleasure, I was the smiling victim of her wanton sexual hunger and there was no action I could, or would, or should, take to prevent her seeking complete and total satisfaction.

Following this night of matchless sexual nirvana that I will not sully with renderings into purple prose, the pain-to-pleasure balance was most irregular. Short of asking her "please stop taking me to the pinnacle of sexual paradise, for this will upset the delicate balance of the columns", there was no option except to farm the consequences to the near future. When the evening was over, once I had recovered basic motor skills, I updated the ledger:

Pleasure	Pain
Kisses from the lips of Eros, Cupid, and Christina Hendricks combined into one sweet mouth	It stopped.
Fellatio++	
Soixante-neuf + Soixante-neuf = Cent trente-huit	

Pleasure	Pain
Five hours of sensorially indescribable intercourse where every sinew, nerve ending, and muscle shuddered with pleasure horrific in its scope and majesty	
Cent trente-huit + Cent trente-huit = Deux cent soixante-seize	

To achieve redress, I concentrated on the length of each sexual act, rather than assessing the pleasure contained in each (the fact the pleasures were unbounding and stratospheric would render this somewhat futile, however, I was committed to maintaining an illusion of balance). We had uninterrupted coitus for most of the night, with breaks in between each orgasm for catching breath and sweating out the bliss. In total, we experienced about five hours of consistent sexual pleasure without suffering (though I observed audible neck-cricking during the first soixante-neuf).

I required five hours' uncut anguish for balance. To achieve this, I rented the last two *Pirates of the Caribbean* films and skipped breakfast and lunch. This was a suitable horror, but pleasure was still rippling through the very core of my being like a sine wave rippling through the nocturnes of Mr. Chopin. I felt like the luckiest man on the planet and that nothing could shunt me from my throne. How was I supposed to realign my ledger?

For our next date, I made a series of punitive sartorial choices to secure sensations of extreme tightness, chafing, and thrombosis at each point where fasteners collided with flesh. The first was to tighten my belt to the farthest rung to create a red ring around my hips, the sort of embolic mottling common to erotic contortionists trussed up on crossbars for hours at a time. I wore undersize anti-shoes, curling up each toe to make walking a perpetual ouchie on each paving slab. I tied a tie so tight that strong exhalations caused a bronchial wheeze to leak out with the force of a copper kettle achieving full steam. To sabotage her lust, I turned up late smelling of vodka, sweat, and cat food. She was not to be deterred. We ate this time—a predictable slab of oysters and chocolate— then retired to her lair for frenzied humping against the fridge-freezer and other robust erotic shenanigans too XXX for a respectable writer to outline without descending into pits of hardcore.

As we were kissing and warming up for our third session of the evening I reached for a desperate solution.

"Why don't you spank me?" I asked.

"You into that?"

"I've never tried it."

"Bend over."

She smiled, wrinkled her nose, and commenced with painless thwacks across the left cheek—mild and non-punishing naughtinesses that never rose above a wee tingle—until I insisted on a supersonic palm application. She ran across the room and performed a full-palmed thwack-shock across my chosen half of rump, sending the left cheek into a wobble that spread to the right with the seismic magnificence of a tremor feeling up a fault line. She took to this makeshift masochism with vim (she had, I later learned, a rich past of cat-o'-nine-tails kink involving members of Hamilton Accies), retrieving a broom from the cupboard and making an intentional beeline for my upper legs.

I fell to the floor.

"Up, maggot!"

"What?"

Her sudden transformation from cute redhead to R. Lee Ermey was shocking.

My buttocks stinging, I crawled to the couch. I made a courageous decision.

"Stick the broom handle up my posterior," I said.

"Sure?" She paused. Five seconds later she wet her fingers and worked the wooden nub of the broom into my saliva-sopped starfish, making a firm forward in opposition to the protesting sphincter, turning the broom-top to aid a deeper penetration.

I shrieked in pain.

"OK? You *handle* this, LOL?" she asked.

"Yes," I whimpered. "Deeper."

She twisted the brush some more and I was surprised to notice a penis at full mast (mine), which I rubbed until a semi-soothing pleasure countered the agony. After ten long and torturous minutes, I came with tears in my eyes. Ileana handed the brush to me and told me to do the same. "Sure?" I asked. "Sure as milk," she said, whatever that meant. I took the brush and thwacked her across the buttocks with retributive oomph. She shrieked as though receiving a mere hip-tickle, responding with tittering amusement at the increasing speed and violence of each blow. Once the brush was inserted into her behind, she responded with ludicrous moans that indicated immense pleasure, massaging her clitoris as I worked the handle in further. She came within three minutes.

Right. Take a breath. I realise how low-rent this sounds. But with this rectal broomhandling, I had struck the perfect balance between pleasure and pain. From this point onward, all our sexual activities involved an act of masochistic outrage. Ileana was more than keen to indulge me in diverse perversities (I learned later she was ranked fourth in the UK chart of the Most Erotically Ambitious). Her favourite improvised kink involved a brown-baize strap-on dildo, with which she would penetrate me wearing the clothes I had been wearing before I shed the clothes so she could put on the clothes I had been wearing for the purpose of sodomising me while wearing my clothes.

If I felt too much pain had been inflicted of an evening, I would permit Ileana to perform one act of fellatio upon me, with no bites or hard sucks. This proceeded apace, until the balance looked like:

Pleasure	Pain
Anal sex: pleasure shocks from sphincter to cock	Anal sex: repeated stabbing pains and subsequent bruising or bleeding

Pleasure	Pain
Sadomasochism: a prelude to the pleasure to come	Sadomasochism: the pain of being hurt a lot with brooms and whips
Oral sex (kind): the various known pleasures of oral sex	Oral sex (unkind): biting and chewing on penis causes sheer terror

Three weeks later, tired of the endless suck and slap, slurp and thwack, we invited our friends round to handle the workload. If invited and served prawn sandwiches and lemonade, most people will indulge in their darkest perversions. I instructed the invited to run riot in the flat with vacuum cleaners, brooms, and rolltop mops. My friend Roland was overkeen. Before I had time to introduce him to Ileana, he leapt straight into the cupboard, snatched up the Dyson Max Power and chased me around the flat shouting "achtung, baby!", clobbering me about the head, ankles, and chest until I begged for less. Shedding our clothes, he attached the hoover nozzle to my penis and took me to a terrible orgasm on the low suck setting.

The following is a representative sample of the moral ooze into which we sank.

Laurence, an old college friend, arrived in a ballerina costume, his carcass coated in red war paint, and spanked Ileana with a table tennis bat until her buttocks were redder than an embarrassed tomato; Chrissie, Ileana's best friend, screwed me through the television, carving two holes at either end for our wrigglies while a Bon Jovi concert on BBC4 blasted 'Bed of Roses'; Silvia, a Viennese exchange student, crawled around the room indulging her fetish for ankles, slobbering and chewing on each one until the victim shooed her off; Lionel, a chartered accountant, shouted the names of his dead parents as a pale-faced stranger fellated him in a Thatcher wig; Alistair, a retired bus conductor, instructed a Clara Bow lookalike to pour bleach into his anus, shuddering as though receiving the blood of Christ in his alimentary caverns; Harold and Ted, two brothers from Nantwich, had squeezed toothpaste along their erect penises, then instructed Nina and Gina, two sisters from Crieff, to "brush their teeth" along the bulbous scarp of their hardness; Clive, a mixologist and part-time dog walker, liked having the hairs pulled from his buttocks one at a time, a task performed with heart by a haunted-looking croupier in her mid-50s; Andrew, a small-shouldered ex-cop whose preference was for the lash; Milton, an estate agent who loved the bullwhip on charred flesh, and so on.

This ended at some point, as all impromptu erotic collisions must, in a whimper of fluids and snoozing bodies.

To calculate the level of pleasures to pains would require a superhuman effort of recall and a review of the toothmarks, the suction rings, and other cutaneous perforations that had taken place without my bodily consent.

I shooed the stuporous participants from my flat. Some of the more incorrigible propositioned me with mops and toffees, but upon opening the curtains, the harsh sunlight cooled their ardours. Stepping outside for some fresh air, I observed that Ileana's guest list had been larger than I expected—a line of tired people copulated half-asleep in the corridor, this love-chain spilling into the streets, where several couples had furtive sex against the walls as men in raincoats went about their men-in-raincoats business.

I closed the door. In a panic, I wondered if we had triggered a domino effect of non-stop copulative madness, a state of primitive perma-fuck where our preference as a society for private sex had switched to street-bound free love.

Fortunately, we hadn't.

Ileana appeared from the bedroom, stepping over her sleeping brother who had spent the night tonguing whipped cream from the toes of willing and unwilling participants, her face pained from exhaustion, stuck in an orgasmic scowl, coated in a sheen of translucent emissions.

"Oh man, what was that?" she said, falling onto the couch.

"That was a disgrace," I said.

"Mayhap a tad OTT."

"No kidding."

"No sex for nine months, I reckon."

"Or ever."

We slept for ten hours, showered, and cleaned the flat using equip-ment borrowed from our neighbours. We made a pledge that from that moment on, we would remain celibate (for nine months) and live in a state of pleasure-free Amishness until the sleaze wore off.

My ledger? I concluded, with ease, that my experiment had been a pro-found failure, and resigned myself to an imbalance heavily weighted on the side of pleasure.

Downfall of the Dans: A Comic Opera

Anacrusis

S IT TIGHT and await the orchestra. Feet off the seats. Picture an airplane barrelling toward the ground. A liner bound for the iceberg. How a silence, when protracted, builds to a pitch of unbearable tension. Imagine three people in the same workplace being summoned to the Head Office. The curtain rises to polite applause. Dan Trumpet is first to enter. A short staccato, a burst of panic. The boss is holding a hatchet. The orchestra erupts: a stab of flutes, a kick of trumpets. Next, Dan Horn. Ears held captive in a spectacle of sound. The notes enter a repeating C scale, scoping out the danger with a picky piccolo. And last, there's Dan Tuba. The orchestra swells in a crescendo of trembling violins and crashing cymbals. Panic takes flight. The airplane crashes, the liner goes kersplash. Panic ascends the scale as the Dans mooch from the office, catching each other's eye, registering that flash of tuneful dread. A pack of gongs are struck. Once. Twice. The Dans turn to face the orchestra, picking shrapnel from their bloodied knees. This music will sweep them into torpor, into terror, into oblivion. The silence protracts, building to a pitch of unbearable tension. The Dans storm out. An echo rebounds in the stalls. It sounds once, then twice, then is gone. Feet off the seats. The aria awaits.

C

Dan Trumpet is riffling through his rolodex looking for allies. His introvert nature makes him solid backroom material. A useful fulcrum for thriving dotcom companies seeking strong mental support among IT hotshots and whizz-kid number crunchers. It won't be so bad, he thinks, if he can phone up Dan Bassoon at Shepard Tones to ask if there's space for him in his webslinger squad at the Discrete Business Park. The short sullen girl in the marketing department who gave him a come-hither look last week watches him lug his data cleansing software through the office as colleagues weep and howl.

The worst thing about that smug shrug of a boss is he's so hideous, punching him repeatedly would only make him sexier. It's not like he's bothered. He's only thirty-four and work is horseshit anyway, and it's not as if Jan can't tide him over for a few months, keep the kids fed and that, help him through a bad patch. Up with the system! The recession might be in full-swing and there might be no room for Dan Horn, but so what? It's the perfect time to read more books and learn karate and get blotto. He's not worried.

Pardon me . . . you're screwed. Introducing Mr. Dan Tuba, the tramp. Have you met Dan Tuba? He raids bins and sucks slugs for nourishment. Then eats them. Then throws up. Then eats them again. You're screwed. Are McDonalds hiring? Is it so hard? "Would you like ketchup with that?" Don't they have ketchup at the tables? Or do you have to provide your own? What is dignity, anyway? At least at McDonald's you can steal chips. You're screwed. What now? Breathe. What now? Keep breathing. Go to McDonald's. What . . . now? No, sell your kidneys first. Yes, now! Go now! You're. Screwed.

D

\# Turns out there are no thriving dotcom companies looking for a back-room fulcrum. The dotcom companies are content with their thriving workforce of one. Two for the big enchiladas. (Someone to make the coffee). Turns out that short sullen girl reported him to the Head Office for "lascivious looks" over the printer and his redundancy pay has been suspended. Oh well. He can always phone Dan Oboe at the IT Fixers and secure some grunt work humping processors for bigwigs. It won't be so bad, he thinks, if he has to shuck some boxes for a while. Get some exercise!

\# Right. Jan's been sacked too. It's not like she's bothered. But she doesn't know he's been sacked too. So he's bothered. And soon she will be. Bothered. Their adorable son, Tim, isn't bothered. As far as he's concerned Daddy (Dan-o-matic) and Mummy (The Mummy) are fine and nothing isn't fine. It's all fine, that's the line. There's another line—at the Jobcentre—where mummy and daddy stand in the daytime. How hard can it be to find work in a massive month? It's not like there's, like, no jobs anywhere, is there? Time to reflect. Read *Gorillas in the Mist*.

\# McDonalds aren't hiring. Not. Bloody. Hiring. Have you met Dan, the actual tramp? He would like fries with that but can't afford them. Or the burger. Or bap. Do something, Dan. Dan the Man. Do something. Don't sit there biting your nails and licking your wounds, Dan! What is lower than McDonalds? Is there anything lower? OK, so. Get up. Go home. Run a bath. Conserve water. Have something to eat. But no treats. This is wartime, and in wartime, we ration. We sit in the dark and await the bombs. The bombs are coming Dan. Do you hear them?

E

♭ Perhaps being in the house won't be so bad. He can always interface with the fellers on the technocratic information stream and plant his flag on the moonface of progress. Or watch some TV. He now has time to burn. To exercise, revitalize the Dan Trumpet backroom fulcrum interdependence database, prepare for his sexual harassment lawsuit. It's not as if he was *that* rough with her in the cupboard that time, and she was asking for it anyway. She's probably envisioning a bankruptcy ruination personality destruction scenario. Well, no time to sit around. Back to pumping dry the data wells!

♭ Time to regroup. It's not like they've lost their house. Yet. I mean, Jan shouldn't have screamed at the benefits officer like that. Or the police officer. But so what? They won't have any money coming in. Right. They might lose their house, but it's not like they're starving. I mean, he shouldn't have punched the benefits officer. Or the police officer. But who can say, hands up, they've never broken someone's nose by mistake? It's not like Tim saw much. Well, it's not like he joined in. Lucky he was there to give the men a tissue. Little star.

♭ Daniel, are you listening? Or is that wax build-up back in your lugs? Didn't you have them syringed last time, buddy? Shouldn't you, perhaps? Or perhaps you really are a fecking twit. Did you really think you could earn money *busking*? Daniel? Danny, me old mate? Really? You can't even play the ukulele, sonny! Anyway, you'd think playing opposite the music shop you stole it from would be a foolhardy move. Wouldn't you? The bombs are magnificent, Daniel. When the bombs erupt in your blood it's like an orgasm, isn't it, Daniel? Ever had one of those? ORGASM. Never mind.

F

In his mind, there's nothing rude about surfing the viral netbase on his phone during the trial. Can't sit by and let the progress-munchers nab his piece of the commercial pie, can he? He *is* listening. To parts. He hears his legal aid praise his strongest characteristics—courteous, a strong backroom fulcrum, often semi-pleasant. He is too busy datalinking with a contingent of Nepalese financiers about a possible dotcom discovery among netbookers, or whatever. Something is said about a rape and serious offence and a prison sentence. If he drops his shortfall by a quarter, he could make over £10K!

Losing custody of a son wouldn't be too bad. He'd reclaim him again at some point. It's like losing a set of keys. Awkward at first, then one day they turn up under a pile of folders. Tim would turn up later, under a pile of legal forms. I mean, it might even be *cool* to put the pause on him for a while. Some breathing space. Not that he wouldn't miss the wee squirt, but if he was going to prison for stealing a Ford Focus, he could hardly take him along. Could he? He should ask about that.

Daniel, you are dancing into a nervous breakdown. Daniel, you are dancing into a shopping centre in a pair of blue-chequered M&S boxers with the tag still attached singing 'The Winner Takes It All.' Daniel, you are twatting a police officer with a ukulele and stealing his wallet. Daniel, you are running out the shopping centre into the arms of the law and flailing around like a spinning top and punching policemen in the nostrils and kicking the windows of the car and screaming 'The Winner Takes It *Aaaaalllll*.' Daniel, you are not a winner, Daniel. You have nothing. Daniel.

G

\# No laptops permitted in prison cells. How was he supposed to interface? What sort of online fulcrum functions without a constant chainlink of factoids and datoids? There was nothing to do in here except *think*. How could he expect to think when he didn't have the proper means: his database?

\# Solitude wasn't so bad. It's not like there was a hairy rapist in his bunk. There *was* a hairy man in his bunk, but he was 50% sure he wasn't a rapist. It's not like he asked. But rapists didn't chew their nails like that or mumble about digital interfaeces. Or look strangely familiar. Tim was probably fine. I mean, he was probably crying and terrified. But underneath, he'd be fine. He was strong. Well, he wasn't *actually* strong. He cried at a dead fly, but he'd survive. Jan was probably OK too, probably having oodles of chuckles in the women's prison. They probably showered together and had frolics. Might have been nice to go there with her, ha ha. Mealtime soon. Good. He's starving.

\# Look what happened, Daniel. "So what?" So, can't you see how foolish you are? "You hardly helped." I'm an observer. A commentator, Daniel. "Stop calling me Daniel. It's Dan." Ooh, touched a nerve, have I? "All you do is undermine me, and it's driving me insane." Bit late for that, Dan . . . ee-yell. You're already banged up, facing a long sentence. "I'll plead insanity. I don't care anymore." A nihilist now, are we? "Shut up." Take my advice, Dan. Befriend the screws. Do them favours, they'll do you favours. I mean sexual, Dan. Sexual favours. "You want me to screw the screws?" Clue's in the name, Dan. Yell. "Well, maybe you should shut up." Wow, that's quite the putdown, buddy! Only trying to help . . . "Dan." Yell.

A

That was it. Without a network of opportunities on a suprainformational panglobal überbyte panoramaface there was no reason to exist. How was he supposed to interact with the blankness of silence, how could he carve his slice of progress pie from the cakes of despair? He couldn't. He could not.

He made a friend. The strongest man in the prison, his friend could lift tables above his head while fending off four guards with his toes. And from the looks of him, this wasn't a boast. Sure, he might have used him as a punching bag a few times, but these were rites of passage, he assumed. He'd made a friend. A friend that threatened to track down Tim and tear out his eyes if he ever let on to the fuckpigs that he was dealing skag in the showers. But a friend, still. He got a discount on skag for keeping his mouth shut and for helping him through the long nights when he needed someone to hold. He missed Jan sometimes. Only sometimes.

Daniel! "I need to sort this out." Daniel! "Things can't go on like this." Daniel! "I mean, look at me. What happened to me? I'm sacked and I have a breakdown." Daniel! "Now I'm in prison. I mean, something has to change." Daniel! "Something in me has to change." Daniel! "But who can help me? Who can I turn to?" *Daniel*! "Who could possibly help me?" Daniel! "Oh God . . . it's God, isn't it? I knew this day would come!" *Daniel*! "I have to ask Him for guidance. For too long I've been running from Him." *Daniel*! "Why did it take me so long to realise this? He's been waiting for me all this time. Waiting for my love, to save my fat sinner's soul." *Daniiieeeeeeeeeeeel*!

B

♭ He lives in a disconnected world. A man unplugged. Lost in the main-frame of reality. He was looking at ten years offline, shut in a box of exclusion with no means of accessing vital supplements on the informational matrix. There was nothing left for him to do. Well, one thing.

♭ OK, he misses Jan most of the time. The longing sometimes is atrocious. Good days and bad days. Mainly bad days. Being his friend's sexual bear is hard, degrading work. Still, it keeps the screws off his back. And he'll be reunited with Jan soon. Bet she was having fun.

♭ Why won't you speak to me, Dan? "Lord, I am sorry for what I have done and the life I have led. I hope you can forgive me in time. I am willing to work with you towards being a better person. Towards a re-demption. I have been living a lie for so long and I am ready to accept you into my bosom at last." Your *bosom*? Dan, don't shut me out. "It's this voice in my head that has ruined me and driven me mad, this voice of the Devil. If I can kill him forever, I'll be free, and I can love at last." Listen to yourself, Dan. You sound like a mental patient. "There are two things I want to achieve in life. One is to find a plateau of contentment and kindness, the other is to help others like me survive the abyss, to redeem themselves from shame and sin." Oh, for the love of . . . "God. I'm not asking much. All I ask is that you accept me and perhaps one day I'll be worthy of your love and understanding." Oh, for . . . Dan, you pillock, you ape, you . . . Daniel . . . "One day at a time, Lord."

C

Dan secures his belt around the light and steps into the noose. He en-visions a clear drop-down fast-choke minimum pain-in-death scenario, but a second overview shows a more plausible slow-choke fall-and-break-

legs outcome, a less desirable shortfall. But this was a crisis point. He would have to grin and bear it.

Dan steps out the prison cell into a drizzly afternoon. The guards promise it's Thursday and the screws are certain it's Monday, honest. Jan is waiting for him at the gate with Tim. They don't look pleased to see him, but they've been through hell themselves. Not that they're bothered.

Dan kneels at the altar and feels nothing. His conversion in prison had been born of desperation and the need to connect with someone or suffer the humiliation of the Devil. It wasn't a simple case of talking to a priest and spilling his guts and basking in the divine light of redemption. He had to show he was willing to change his ways. He finds the police officer he'd assaulted and tries to apologise, only to have the door slammed in his face. He apologises to the manager of the shopping centre where he suffered his breakdown. He takes himself to his family and apologises for the shame and discomfort he caused. They turn him away. Having suffered enough he turns to God once more. He feels the need to believe. To keep the Devil behind bars. Breathing in the cool morning air he feels a warmth opening inside him and decides to perform random acts of kindness. They aren't always accepted with good grace (practically dragging old ladies across the road) but most people are satisfied (with the cash handouts). Although Dan knows he won't work again for the next four years, he's content. Edging nearer to peace.

D

He hangs from the light, choosing a long-term unconscious dead-as-a-doornail pushing-up-daises strategy. He wasn't much good at living outside the digital interface. Whatever awaits him on the other side, he hopes they have broadband access and a coaxial flex adaptor with USB attachment sticks. This is his idea of bliss.

\# Back home. Pizza in the oven and *The Incredibles* on DVD. Time to take the reins of domestic life and dramatically return to relaxing and lounging about and not caring very much. Sitting on the sofa with Jan and Tim and heckling the TV. This is his idea of bliss.

\# He sits in silence and listens to the night noises: the soft whoosh of traffic and the calming trickle of rain. The stillness of things brings him closer to God. He sends a dream of happiness into the night and prays for world salvation. This is his idea of bliss.

Coda

And so, as the curtains fall, the violins sound a haunting lament for the figure of Dan hanged in his prison cell. The audience sit, teeth-clenched in horror, hoping for a happier climax. A foreboding silence. The final flames dying in the plane. The last few bubbles popping on the surface. From the gloom comes a soft piccolo, playing in major key. The curtain rises. This is Dan and Jan's theme. A ten-note ode to the smooth-sailing ship of domestic happiness. There is light applause as the tone lifts from existential dread to redemptive pleasure. This is confirmed by the rising organ notes, striking a profound chord with the audience whose skin is prickling and whose hearts are thumping. This is Dan's theme. His conversion and complete fulfilment furnishes the audience with hope. Perhaps there is something to be said for living a purer and simpler life. Perhaps what truly makes us happy are our smaller interactions with the world. Perhaps we can take off again into the skies, set sail on a liner into the sunset. Perhaps if we come together as people, united in love in happiness, we can make a difference. Maybe this feeling will stay with us when we leave the theatre. Perhaps it's a nice sentiment, but more the stuff of fiction than real life. The curtain descends. Show's over.

ATTENTION!

THE FOLLOWING *is a transmission from the Subspecies Control Bureau. It has come to our attention certain rebel groups have been faking their heterosexual relationships to attain cheap housing as couples in the Safe District. We will not tolerate homosexuals posing as heterosexuals and we will not house couples faking mutual pheromonal affections.*

What follows is a warning to those thinking about tricking the system. Men: please follow the narrative on the left. Women: the narrative on the right. Read these words carefully. There are no exemptions from the rules. DO NOT LIE TO THE STATE. End of message.

The MAN threw a Kleenex on the urine-soaked lino in the toilets at Pizza Hut, LONDON. His fulsome chest looked so perfect in the hot pepperoni moonlight that Francis—a _{man} paid to lick the floor clean—leapt to retrieve the tissue for this handsome MALE specimen.

The WOMAN stood in demure disobedience on the SOHO pavement and hailed a taxi with a microtwitch of her pinkie. Across the street, Frances—a _{woman} semaphoring hard to summon the same taxi—noticed the silken allure of the WOMAN and aborted her attempt.

"You are kind, yet you belong to a subspecies I cannot tolerate," the MAN said, rubbing the tissue into Francis's amazed face.

"I will take this taxi and you can have the privilege of a burned cheek," the WOMAN said, stubbing her cigarette on Frances.

Error! *Scrawny legs. A sheepish languor in my gait. Unworthiness.*

Error! *Simpering. Lurching like a fool. Unworthiness.*

Fighting to suppress a wave of panic, Francis fled the Pizza Hut and took manic leaps across the street, cursing his inferiority (in respectfully hushed tones) until he . . .

Her cheek stinging from the fiery ash, Frances salved the pain by slapping herself in the face and running into the wind, letting the whoosh soothe her burns until she . . .

. . . collided into another, almost scraping the paintwork of a super-sheened Vauxhall Mokka.

"I am so sincerely sorry," they said unison.

"Forgive me, I was not trying to steal this important car," they said, again in unison. This simultaneous exchange of identical words was humorous, satirising their standardisation as a human subspecies. They permitted themselves two furtive chuckles, mindful of the offence for men and women to be seen laughing near an important car. They hastily parted.

In his hovel low in the LONDON wilds, Francis ate a wasp and roach sandwich and worried about the woman with whom he had collided. Might she have been a mole for the Subspecies Control Bureau and viewed him a threat to the status quo? If so, he might lose his hovel, food entitlement, and risk instant downgrading to a boy. He couldn't relax.

Picking the loosest lice from his beard, he formed a plan of action. He would relocate the woman and kidnap her, then replace her brain with a specimen from the corpse dump.

Error! *How the hell do I find her?*

Returning to the streets, Francis considered two options—the kennel for MEN (where the concubines worked) or in a woman's shelter. If the former, she could not leave for another month. There was no choice except to assume the latter.

The night was bleached in torrid ochre. Toxic vapours swaddled Francis as he ventured between male and

In her corner of the woman's shelter, Frances nibbled on a sixth of bread after splashing lukewarm tap water on her burn. Might that man have been an undercover doctor with a soothing balm on his person for her ailing cheek? If so, she might not lose her place at the Tofu Express for being too hideous to be seen serving the MEN and WOMEN.

If she could find the man again and bribe him with her food ration for the week, she might convince him to repair her face. She had four slices of bugless bread and a cat spleen to spare.

Error! *How the hell do I find him?*

She wandered at random to the wilds, a savage slumland where men foraged for scraps and positions in the ADULT world. If she sidestepped the shards of moonlight, she would avoid vicious organ poaching by feral boy hunters.

Lurking parallel to the illumined paths, she headed towards the demarcation line. She buttoned

_{female} districts to the breeding border, where starved metasexuals lived unbound like muzhiks.

Upon arrival at the border, across from a pair of mating foxes, Francis was surprised to see . . .

her coat and bunched her hair under a bobble hat, hoping to pose as a _{man.}

Upon arrival at the border, across from a pair of mating foxes, Francis was surprised to see . . .

". . . is that you?" they asked, squinting in the non-light.

"I came expressly to seek you," they said.

Frances paused.

Francis smiled.

"We should speak one at a time," he said.

"Yes. Perhaps as a courtesy, you might explain why you tried to find me?" she asked.

"I will. First, I think we should remove ourselves from these mating foxes to reduce the prospect of terminal ankle wounds."

"Yes, I concur."

Concealing themselves behind a skip, rank with the odour of half-chewed cats and smelted metals oozing unwanted condensates, Frances and Francis could talk with a lower risk of bloodshed. Paranoia took hold in Francis with switch-like swiftness. He lunged for Frances and pressed his hand round her neck and pinned her with a violent shove against the skip.

"I apologise for the force. I must ask if you an agent from the Subspecies Control Bureau. Was I followed?"

"No, I am not," Frances said, calm and choking. "I thought you might be an undercover doctor."

"A doctor?"

"Yes. A WOMAN stubbed her cigarette on my right cheek earlier when I relinquished for her a cab."

Francis loosened his hold. It was evident from her shaking hands and the crimson scab on her cheek that her explanation had credence. This in addition to the absence of reinforcements swooping in from the blackness to set about reducing his organs to crow fodder.

"I apologise, I . . . "

Frances shot back to the demarcation line with the spasmic retreat of a chronically whipped poodle. She watched the man's violence receding from his clenched hands to his legs, where he gave the skip a macho kick. A plague of bothered rats echoed within the mouldering cat-dump, their high-pitched cries merging with the sad stateless mating of the metasexuals.

"Your reason for seeking me?" Frances asked. Francis fondled the switchblade in his pocket, scanning the woman's high-alert mien.

"Thought an agent had scoped me."

"I see. If I had been an agent?"

"I— "

"The switchblade was to carve out a portion of my brain?"

Francis laughed.

"Yes. I was intending to remove your entire brain from your cranium and surrender your tissue to the night."

"I understand. You are from the wilds?"

"Yes. Beside the Bolus of Great Regret."

"That is where the obsolete men are burned?"

"Yes."

"Is the stench not intolerable?"

Francis inhaled a waft of post-ionic air from the breeding border— a lung-stinging peasouper with an impressive selection of slow-acting carcinogens—cleaner than the air of the wilds.

"Yes. I manage. Listen, I'm not a doctor, but I could treat that burn."

She stood without protest as he inspected the hot scorch of her cheek and, using the tissue from his earlier humiliation, applied a squirt of Pain Evader from the tube in his pocket, and patted the area. Frances winced as the alcohol stung then salved her painful wound.

"I should leave now. Sorry for the misunderstanding."

"That's all right."

"Take care upon returning."

"Thank you."

In his hovel, he brooded on the meeting. To escape poverty, he required an official wife. Having her accepted by the Subspecies Relocation Board meant a place in a safehouse. After a few months, his name would be placed on a housing ladder, taking him (eventually) to the ranks of the underclass.

The long stretch of scrounging and fighting among the misaligned and unauthorised at the lowest social rung had taken its toll. He would have married sooner were it not for one problem—his homosexuality.

Since the ADULT world claimed the right to sexual selection as their own exclusive concept, homosexuals on the fringes were hunted for semen, teeth, and spleens. They lived their lives in the shadows—unseen little insects spreading vice, disease, and terror within cracks in the pavement.

Taking this woman for a wife, he could liberate himself from a life of honest skulking and snarling in poisonous fronds and surrender to a life-long lie in heated rooms. The choice between self-acceptance and self-denial no longer seemed obvious.

Error! *How can I find her this time?*

The wilds crackled with petrochemical flair. Francis, seizing this instance, this rare collision, this last-ditch lunge for future security, understood the risks. Returning to the cat-curdled skip on the border, he was startled to find . . .

Frances splashed water on her cheek to neutralise the acid burn of the Pain Evader. It was obvious the lotion had long expired and was now a pain agitator. Regardless, her interaction with the man had been an unexpected scene with a pleasant ending. The last man she met wanted to harvest her kidneys.

She understood the importance of auditing each human interaction to see whether the merest sliver of self-advancement through association was possible. The answer in this case— perhaps.

Her cheek singed with no speedy heal possible, Tofu Express was sure to void her contract or relegate her to scraping scat from the ovens. Her tormentors in the kitchen, coveting her waitress position, would relish the sight of her scraping mould with her fingernails.

The conclusion was curt: something must bloom from her interaction with the man. The risk of meeting another organ harvester was acceptable. Losing a minor internal was preferable to months of torture from vile women in a squalid kitchen.

Error! *Of what possible use . . . ?*

Tightening the hood of her cagoule to the strictest tog, she retraced her steps through the moonlight outskirts, leaping over a clasp of spent metrosexual orgiasts with a mixture of paranoia and anticipation, startled to find . . .

" . . . it's you."

Francis circled Frances.

Frances circled Francis.

"Well," Francis said, scratching his unburned cheek, "what now?"

The ask struck them like an uppercut . . . presupposing that the future might ever accommodate them. Serene silence, a mutual acceptance of their undefined connection followed until a flutter of flittermice menaces approached from the neckline of the sky, ravenous, black.

"Take cover," Frances shouted. Fleeing the skip's respite, as the flittermice menaces flew in oblique bomb-forage for cat meat, the two were forced to take shelter in the fronds of Rape Forest.

"Bastards!" Francis said.

"Quiet or we'll wake the rapists."

"Sorry," Francis whispered.

At various points in the forest feral men with permanent erections stomped around looking for bodies to violate.

"You returned."

"Yes. I have a proposition of mutual benefit. I require a wife to acquire a place in the safehouse, and a route toward accommodation with working locks and windows. I suggest we pair up as pretend man and wife and fictionalise ourselves into the underclass. Thoughts?"

"That is—"

"I posit that neither of us have much fondness for our lives of ritual debasement. I tried fighting in the rebellion, but our opponents met our violence with laughter. If we acquire accommodation we can at least complete our pointless lives in relative comfort. Thoughts?"

"Yes, I would like to," Frances said, stunned at the suddenness of the prospect, "however, there are a series of rigorous tests to prove mutual affection. The punishment for failure is severe."

"We can pass these tests. It's the same as everything else in the ADULT world. It's a bureaucracy . . . they're more concerned with pleasing superiors and minimising hassle than the truth. If we learn everything there is to know about each other, and memorise the details, we can secure our place."

Frances wasted no time in accepting the proposition. She nodded in assent and offered her hand.

"Nice to meet you. I'm Frances," she said.

Francis snorted.

"I'm Francis."

"With an E?"

"No, an I."

"Nice to meet us, France-is."

He sketched his childhood in the ADULT homes before the Social Reorder, his schooling in the wilds, his stretch fighting for social equality, his present as a servant in LONDON restaurants.

He recounted the time he captured a MAN, stripped him bare and bludgeoned him with a lump of theralite—the sorriest night of his life. He memorised Frances's details carefully.

"One more thing," he said . . .

She sketched her childhood moving from shack to shack, her homeschooling and parents' suicide pact, her adolescence in the orphanage and relocation to $_{women}$'s shelters.

She spoke honestly and emotionlessly, recounting the time her mother was raped by rebel $_{boys}$. As Francis spoke, she repeated each fact over and over in her mind.

"One more thing," she said . . .

. . . "I'm a homosexual."

Savages shrieked in the distance.

Taking no time to reflect on the fortuitousness of the coincidence, the pair braved the smog to reach the Subspecies Relocation Board in SOHO. The walk lasted several hours, leaving them ample time to memorise a sequence of intimate recollections to simulate long-time coupling. The building had a sheet metal roof and evidence of attempted arson on the ex-white frontage, and plasterboard tagged with PPP, the mark of the quashed resistance. A hundred-strong line of incongruous couples stood outside in a phalanx of competing queues—last-ditch opportunists with the same motive as themselves.

"Look at all these people," Frances said.

"It's OK. We're prepared. These chisellers will not have rehearsed."

The four-hour wait was cold and chairless. Inside rooms contoured to provide the least stimulating sensorial experience, with antiseptic airless bunker-like chambers modelled on the enhanced interrogation rooms at Abu Gharib, the couple were separated and made to complete questionnaires on each other for phase one of the authentication process. Phase two was to cross-check the information provided by each person in separate interrogation rooms with swapped scrutinisers. The range of knowledge a person retains on a partner is not as vast as one might assume—most people retain a moderate spread of facts on the other, as their persistent presence prevents them from having to commit them to memory.

Their results were 86% 'probable correctness'—one percent lower was an immediate fail—so the final test beckoned. This was a setback neither Francis nor Frances could have anticipated—the Intimacy Test. The scrutiniser led them to a small room where they were instructed to make love to prove they were a proper couple and not homosexuals seeking to exploit the system.

In a quick-thinking move, the two moved towards the bed and curled themselves into a reverse spoon. Frances whispered into Francis's ear:

"This won't work. We have to confess."

"Relax," Francis said, rubbing her back. "We can do this. Think of your freedom."

"I'm a virgin, Francis."

"Yes, so am I."

Francis peered into the observation window, picturing the men with clipboards noting each erotic manoeuvre. He turned to the clinical white walls and linoleum, feeling a sharp tack of

Frances had never been in a position to explore her sexuality. She knew the glamorous WOMEN aroused something dangerous inside her, something exclusive and dark. She turned panic on top of the stab of fear and the knife of anxiety.

It was a matter of improvisation. He took Frances's head in his hands, caressed her hair, mouthed *it's OK*, and attempted a kiss. She recoiled at first, then helped keep the illusion going.

After a minute's kissing, making lustful noises to indicate passion, he moved onto the bed, where he manufactured a passionate assault across her body . . .

to face the stranger for whatever came next.

Francis kissed her with clumsy violence. She grabbed his arm, drawing him against her. The whole episode was for show, but she had no choice but to perform if she wanted her freedom.

If she performed this act, she would be done with the poverty, the hunger, the abuse. She carried this precious thought with her to the bed . . .

The caressing and rubbing proceeded with the violence of a murderer scrubbing the victim's blood from their bodies. It was apparent that the notion of achieving arousal in these clinical circumstances with the MEN watching them behind the mirror was the stuff of dreams. Francis began unbuttoning his clothes, paused for a moment to steel himself not to faint, and unbuttoned Frances's clothes.

Undressed, naked, they embraced. Francis tried to arouse himself thinking about hot soup, radiators, and a bed with an actual mattress. He clasped Frances and whispered in her ear:

"Think of the washing machine. Think of the door with a lock," he said.

"Yes," Frances said.

As foreplay, this was something of a mistake. Francis tried picturing an attractive MAN lounging on a comfortable sofa while kissing his way around Frances's body. Frances imagined the sultry WOMAN who had stubbed her cigarette out on her cheek in a heroic attempt to prepare herself for penetration. These images failed to propel them through the awkward grapple with each other's bodies to a state of readiness for the coital act.

In an era when innocence was obsolete and corruption was the norm, the two underwent a strange regression to childhood. Rather than performing ADULT lovemaking, the two reclaimed their adolescence from the Social Reorder—the moment men became MEN and women became WOMEN, and men became ₘₑₙ and women became ᵥₒₘₑₙ.

Locked together in a fusion of wholly confected memories—of innocent frolics in meadows, of kisschasing around apple trees—the two held and patted and played with each other like the children they never were. There was no penetration. There was nothing except a weak simulation of the feelings of ADULTS.

After, their bodies were swabbed for the requisite fluids.

One of the scrutinisers, holding a clipboard, entered the room and paused for effect.

He said:

"You have been unsuccessful. You have one minute to leave the premises. You will receive your punishment in due course. You are not entitled to another chance."

This has been a transmission on behalf of the Subspecies Relocation Board. Do not practice mendacity in your dealings with us or the consequences will be serious. There can be no deception in the sacred annals of government. Take onboard this lesson and only make claims that are 100% genuine. Consider this a friendly warning. End of transmission.

Violent Solutions to Popular Problems

INTERROGATOR: Please outline the nature of the problem.

Man: I have, for the last three years, been tormented by squatters in my riverside villa.

Int: Elaborate lightly.

Man: When the Ghent to Vesuvius transeuropean pipeline—a twelve billion-euro build on which I had acted as Chief Overseer—was complete, I treated myself to a luxury villa nestling on the banks of the River Dee.

Int: Why do pretty things always 'nestle' beside rivers? Would a washed-up corpse 'nestle' lovingly on the banks, for instance?

Man: It's an expression.

Int: Yes, I'm calling into question the expression's validity. But please continue.

Man: Right. Well, I acquired the villa, nestling or otherwise by the River Dee, the one in Aberdeenshire. By the time I was ready to take my well-earned R&R with my wife Merry, my realtor informed me that four squatters had "taken" the property, using my home to establish an enormous social media campaign on the rights of the well-heeled to loan their properties rent-free to the muck-spattered tinker class. Naturally I unleashed my legal militia, assuming they would be removed in a whisker and that Aberdeenshire County Council would reimburse me for the cleaning costs and trauma suffered.

Int: And that didn't happen.

Man: No. Such was the popularity of this campaign that the squatters had raised enough to marshal a robust legal rebuttal, who among them had unearthed an obscure county law stating that whomsoever decreeth can stayeth on mine landeth, etcetera.

Int: This was Ploughman's Decree unrevised since 1170, applicable to a mere twelve hectares of land, on which only your villa happened to nestle.

Man: Yes.

Int: I have here the decree: *Whomfomever wandereth acroff field nor fayre, upon finding ruftic fanctuary, may avail themfelvef of the dwelling therein for af long af it taketh them to find fpiritual refpite.*

Man: Something like that. The snarling beanbag socialists on Twitter roared with laughter, celebrating one in the eye for this pesky Croesus with his sinister riverside property that was somehow symbolic of all the world's ills.

Int: As I understand it, you made your fortune exporting shale gas cheaply from eastern Europe, in contravention of EU contamination directives?

Man: As I have said many times, show me a successful man who amassed his wealth by blindly obeying the rules, and I will show you a watermelon speaking Mandarin. The Zuckerberg Principle, "move fast and break things", has always been the mantra of the ambitious businessman, and once your power is immutable, you'd be a fool not to mobilise serried ranks of lawyers to handle the fines and commence the stonewalling. It's how the world works.

Int: Yes, how naïve of me. So your squatters were, in effect, deploying these very same tactics, remaining in your villa legally, blocking you from a speedy legal slapdown, thus depriving you of the chance to either sell up or nestle on holiday.

Man: My attempts to have them swiftly removed were, alas, unsuccessful. I was advised to humbly step from the shadows and make a televisual plea.

Int: Lovebomb the booers?

Man: Until that point, my image had only appeared in the pages of muckraking rags like Private Eye or Byline Times, showing me as a shifty tyrant on the make, icily staring into cameras while entering important skyscrapers to ruin thousands of lives. So, to counter this, I appeared on a breakfast programme to humanise my kind, as when conman Nick Moran tried courting popularity on Channel Four's The Big Breakfast. My stylist helped me create an effective everyman outfit—casual slacks, tieless shirt, ruffled hair, that sort of thing—to present the image of friendly country chap one may find frequenting a village pub sipping a pint of stout.

Int: The Big Breakfast?

Man: It was a 1990s morning television programme featuring a range of carnival colours and stupendously unfunny hosts.

Int: I see.

Man: In my plea to the viewer, I explained that I had worked myself up from very little (aside from the two or three million seed capital from father, which naturally I neglected to mention) to develop a humble little empire. To appear less villainous, I explained that I had proposed to my partner Merry by the River Dee, and purchased the property as a thank you for her standing by me while I battled testicular cancer while watching my poor mother succumb to Alzheimer's and my sister suffer a second miscarriage.

Int: I'm sorry to hear that.

Man: Well, I'd overegged my pudding. Two distortions of the truth work in tandem. A third can seem like an appeal for pity. In my case, the cancer was actually a mild rash, the Alzheimer's was my mother forgetting to send me flowers on my name day, and the miscarriage was my sister losing her antique brougham carriage that she purchased to help traverse our family estate in an equine fashion. But the public weren't convinced.

Int: This is when you chose your preferred remedy.

Man: Yes. In hindsight, I suspect my solution was rather oh-tee-tee, as they say. I sent the squatters a border collie as a "peace offering". Secured to the belly of that border collie was a small piece of Semtex, which I used to explode the squatters all up the walls. I calculated that repairing the mess caused by the explosion would be cheaper than this continual courtroom battle, in addition to an apology donation to the RSPCA for my "accidental" collie blast, blaming the dog seller for not informing me of the Semtexed belly beforehand.

Int: I see.

Man: Thanks to my careful network, there was no way to trace the Semtex back to me, or indeed to the fictitious dog seller, so the incident was written off as a random spontaneous canine combustion, caused by an accidental leaking of kerosene into his meaty chunks. The renovations took such a long time, my wife decided to sell the property and pick up a far more scenic pied-à-terre in Jersey instead. The River Dee property had accrued millions from the publicity campaign, so we pocketed a nice little nest egg in the end.

Int: How lovely for you. Thank you for your time this afternoon.

Man: My pleasure.

2

Interrogator: Please outline the nature of your problem.

Man: I was employed by Her Majesty's Government to explore the problem of allowing ordinary members of the public to have a vote in national and local elections.

Int: A biggie.

Man: Indeed. The issue was that too many completely ill-informed people were electing to vote in entirely the wrong ways. Ordinarily, our party encourages people to pay scant attention to politicians and take their opinions from our client newspapers, a technique that usually nudges us over the line to a parliamentary majority, but for some reason, voters weren't voting the way our newspapers were telling them to.

Int: That's *horrible*.

Man: Yes, quite. So, we had to solve this thorny Rubik's. Our only real option was to somehow weed the electorate, or rather, weed that portion of the electorate who had no interest in for voting us. We'd suffered a blow post-pandemic, accidentally killing ten of thousands of our voters by accidentally allowing them to catch Covid in nursing homes by accidentally forgetting to protect them. As a result of that polling blow, I was tasked to come up with an innovative new way of turning voters against each other.

Int: Of course.

Man: My first brainwave was to wage a war on chips. To create the idea that middle-class lefties considered chips—sliced potatoes, not fragments of rock—an indicator of stupidity, commonness, and general proletarianism. To wage a war on chips, to accuse luvvie lefties of preferring potato dauphinoise or sweet potato fries or some other poncier staple, was to wage on a war on the soul of the everyman.

Int: Genius. Probably.

Man: We bought two hundred thousand bots from the Vladivostok Internet Agency and bot-bombed the socials, starting with the Twitter hashtag #ChipHaters, chaining them to the hashtags #lefties and #middleclass to make it clear who the real enemies were, i.e. the chip-shunning elitist lefties. This was completely useless.

Int: Oh?

Man: Sadly, we underestimated the propensity of the gnashing masses to swallow this piece of meat unquestioningly. It was roundly ridiculed. That's when I magicked a boffo notion. I had the Prime Minister announce that a fifth Covid vaccine was mandatory to prevent a new Nicaraguan strain from killing off those who barely survived the first four strains. That's when my plan came into effect.

Int: K.

Man: You're very taciturn.

Int: I'm listening in quiet horror as though an aural Sandyhook is taking place in my ears.

Man: That's in bad taste. Righty, so my plan was to implant triggerable explosive particles inside the vaccine, something we developed with the remaining £36.9 billion we had left over from our Test & Trace app. The idea was that everyone in receipt of the vaccine would instantly enrol in a form of extremely localised existential election. The idea was that if enough people voted, anyone in the country could be instantly detonated.

Int: My God.

Man: Genius, no? Evil genius, I concede. That's why they pay me the fat shekels! So once the population were vaccinated, we leaked our real intentions to The Telegraph, blaming a rogue scientist for "misreading" our requests. How it worked was if one hundred people anonymously entered the name and national insurance number of their intended victim into our online request form, the victim received a text message informing them they were scheduled to explode in an hour's time, and to repair themselves to a quiet location.

Int: What if the victim failed to read the message in time?

Man: There were snags with the scheme, I accept. The unfortunate massacre of entire families, offices, and classrooms, was an inevitable teething setback, and one we resolved in the second phase of our app. A text was then sent to everyone *around* the victim warning them of the impending explosion, allowing them ample fleeing time.

Int: What if the victim ran into a crowd?

Man: More teething. In their last ten seconds, several people ran into churches, exploding weddings and funerals, or taking entire pubfuls of people with them in bloody-minded retribution. We resolved this by making it legal for passersby to stun attempted suicide bombers before their time was up, equipping everyone with a taser.

Int: That must have been expensive.

Man: Nah. We still had £36.8 billion leftover.

Int: Continue.

Man: Sure thing. My, you're in a grumpy mood, I must say. By analysing the harvested user data from our affiliated partners, we were able to pinpoint those who had no intention of voting for us, and alerted our followers to their traits. Our trusty lynch mob of seething supporters leapt at the chance to explode the lefties and help us weed the voting public to ensure a solid majority for our party. Of course, a counterinsurgency of lefties activated their frothing keyboard warriors too, but liberal fury is no match for the intolerant right-wing who, in this instance, took 'triggering' to a whole new level, swooping in with vengeance on every bleeding heart and blowing that heart and the surrounding body to pieces.

Int: And how was this electorally?

Man: Sadly, the Anti-Vax Party romped home with 100% of the vote, there being only unvaccinated people left in the country.

Int: What a shame.

Man: I'm all right. I recently started working as head of PR for Glaxo-SmithKline.

Int: Thanks for your time.

Man: Don't mention it. Buck up.

3

Interrogator: Please outline the nature of your problem.

Man: A reader prodded a communiqué toward my ken enquiring re Marilyn Volt. In my second novel *The House of Writers*, Marilyn Volt appears as the building manager of the titular tower, periodically whizzing from floor to floor in a blaze of untethered kook. He was correct in stating that Marilyn Volt is based on a real Marilyn Volt, a Texan who once attended my writing courses at the Arlington Baptist University, where I was recruited errorly in David Nicholls' stead (author of nauseating romcoms, predictably remaindered and silverscreened).

Int: You still haven't outlined with any pith an issue.

Man: I'm creeping therewards. This Volt wrote strangely electrifying sentences of sexual menace, look: *My Christian baby moaning in the corner as the ceiling sweat blood over the lone buttock of a man who had caterwauled his way inside my body.* And this, see: *Sickly plumbed were the depths in that bile-black Sedan, Miriam bound to the bumper as her male enfiladed his seed into her Hellman's Province.*

Int: Fascinating. Could you—

Man: I happened upon her in a non-scholarly setting while bumming round the boutiques of West Arlington in sweatpants and sandals. She was serving in sidestreet café The Wooden Hermit (real name not redacted) and as I entered, my weary peepers observed twelve hunks of beef rowed aloft on copper platers, oozing Belgravian mustard and blood-red cabbage with curls of sourdough coifing across their sinewy lengths. These were the Valentine's Massacres. Rowed above on a copper plater were twelve crabmeat commas, liberally speared with pesto and mince, slathered in ketchup and 46ed in salsa. These were the Parentheseizures. Their architect, Marilyn Volt, smiled in an apron and explained.

Int: You have no problem, do you?

Man: Patience, spooky man! "My lunches are broadsides on the bloat of our contemporary predicament," Volt said. Her oomph was overcharacteristically Texan. "My intention is to serve food so repulsive to the eye and tongue that the eater re-examines the incestuous relationship between food and pharma—the former fattens us up, the latter bills us for diet pills, insulin, and root canal. One man, upon completing my infamous fennel sprawl ribboned with yak meat switched to intravenous feeding for the rest of his days. He's 43% happier."

Int: My hackles are starting to sprout.

Man: I replied: "I'll confess, I had entered this café expecting slicks of cornmeal, patties of horror-meat, and cuboids of botox-creamed Oreos botched onto a bap like some parodically Southern attempt at salad. But these heinous assaults on the anodyne nature of lunch, these surrealistic art installations are a refreshing, post-taste bayonetting of the words yummy and scrumptious and the corporate toxicities of the FSA." Preliminaries kaput, I asked her to the bar-pub.

Int: Hackles at full rise.

Man: Now we come to the problem, you sour-pussed hurrier-upper. At 7pm, the sky shot with streaks of Vittorio Storaro, the air clotting pollen in a hayfeverish frenzy, I met Marilyn Volt at the Pompous Druid. Her unruffled snood made a statement of stunning offensiveness, complimenting her mottoed tote reading DON'T RAPE ME HONEY, I'M ON MY PERIOD. Volt shed ambiguity like a psoriatic lizard her skin. She was well-acquainted with trapping puny college debaters in crushers of their own illogic, bursting them in the blabber of their own stale rhetoric. I found myself a chair and waited until she was seated. Once she was seated (opposite me on a similar chair), I spoke these words. "You have a burning hatred for crimes against digestion," I said. Her outstanding smile erupted across her outstanding face.

Int: Nope, still no problem in sight.

Man: "That is true," she said, "I've been sacked from five restaurants for my culinary broadsides. I started at Max's Bar and Grill by hardboiling a parakeet egg in a sewer of marmalade and provolone, serving the resultant gloop on the faces of the diners. I wanted folks to re-examine the atavism of their mass consumption by awkwardly slurping the burning splat from their foreheads." Thereafter our chat took on a status prosaically known as mythical, as the steel bangle on her wrist shimmied neath the gestural brio of her hands—

Int: Look, if—

Man: Alley-oop, my short-suffering listener, and allow me to apply 2x speed to this narrative. We're both too busy with other forms of fritter to tolerate this novelistic pace-lag, innit?

Int: Yes, whatever that meant.

Man: So, back in the classroom, I continued to rate her stories A+ and urged her to publish everywhere and anywhere, to supplely barge into the literary terrordome with the muscular heft her prose evinced. Instead, she absented. I returned to The Wooden Hermit where I was informed her culinary broadsides had earned her a summary sacking and Twitter fandom. The manager prodded me to the house she shared with several students on Ranch Lane, and when I popped around, I found her in the basement strumming up a stink. "Prof!" she said. (I wasn't a professor, I was falsely impersonating a commercially successful yet artistically deeply unsuccessful author with the same surname, and soon fled before being rumbled and sued). You're the most talented writer on campus, what's with the AWOL?" I asked. "Look over there! That's a freezer. And what's in that freezer? No, wait! Allow me to answer afore you waste your words on fruitless guesses. That freezer, my Scottish emeritus, is filled with aborted foetuses."

Int: What?

Man: Yessee. I blinked. I turned. The basement was packed also with wonky prams, retrieved from Craigslist or local skips or trailer parks. Here's the rest, my whiny opposite. For the sake of re-setting the record re-straight, here it is once more. That evening I accompanied Marilyn Volt as she vroomed her rented van to the homes of seven notorious pro-life headcases, the sort of snide-faced churchy blots responsible for creating the present Texan Gilead. We strode the suburbs holding hands, aping two care-free God-fearing parents, pushing a pram with a rapidly thawing aborted foetus swaddled in acrylic. I casually pushed our pram up the victims' driveway as Marilyn Volt subtly squirted lighter fluid on the unborn babe's non-form, lit a match, then set the pram 'n' foetus ablaze on the doorstep. After, we Hussein Bolted back to the van and drove to the next house.

Int: Wow.

Man: We set all seven ablaze that night, causing satisfying levels of distress to the foetus-fixated hypocrites in their soulless suburban mansionettes. After the last, feral with rebellion, we had passionate sex in the back of her van, humping with an impatience that made our coming strenuously pleasurable. As we lay in a hot melt, our limbs awaking to the speed of the pain inflicted on them, I noticed from the front window police-shaped figures shapily policing toward the van. Marilyn Volt told me to run. She would create a distraction and allow my safe passage back home uncriminalised. I fled the scene as she cartwheeled her naked body in mesmeric loops in the corners of the cops' periphery, creating enough bafflement for me to hide in shrubs 'til dawn. I wheeled my way to Lafayette, Louisiana, and made my nerve-shredding, plane-hopping escape back to Glasgow the next day.

Int: My word.

Man: Worth the wait, no?

Int: Not really.

Man: Marilyn was recently released and has apparently suffered a deficit of oomph.

Int: I didn't ask.

4

Interrogator: Please outline the nature—

Man: Yeah, I know the skinny. My problem was a simple one—how on earth could I land a humiliating punch on a government that operated without shame?

Int: That's meaty.

Man: Isn't it. Beaty, big, and bouncy too.

Int: The Who.

Man: The what? Anyway, let me tell you of my attempt. I wrote a suppressed piece for *The Scotsman* where I visited the Tiki Torches, a private members' club at the House of Commons and an influential lobbying sect that caused conniptions for Prime Minister David Cameron in 2016, when it was revealed by a snoop that the former CEO of Hitachi had pimped David's Corvette to the tune of several thou. I wrote to The Scotsman (no italics, at the editor's request) with a proposal for a scoop, requesting they pay my train fare to London and cover the cost of several nights in a budget Ibis. I had, of course, no experience writing longform journalism for national newspapers, my last few attempts folding into fictional novelettes subsumed by the blizzards of swishy self-aware prose that have become my trademark. This time around, I intended to pen a simple, effective exposé of the backroom rascality taking place in the cocaine-laced hollows of the home of democracy.

Int: Yes, I don't care about that, hurry up.

Man: I plunged into a thicket of subreddits and found a source called bright_eyes, a long-time dropper of inside tittle-tattle, still quaintly wielding an underscore in his various aliases to signal his Old Internet credentials. He informed me that a meeting of the Tiki Torches was taking place at the Suchet Club, an unpopular men-only zone where important blots of nous were imparted in whispers of ale-spray. I made my way straight to the Suchet Club when my train arrived at Euston. Entry to the meeting was simple, as the event had been made public for the last few months.

Int: I had no idea.

Man: Secret channels are where most of the money is made. So, upon entering the Suchet Club, I spotted Michael Gove, a slithery hessian of odium, nobbling truffles from a table of jackanapes noshing canapes. He informed me that the most important issue on the doorstep was the introduction of fines for neon poo artists—these being arty urchins who coat unbagged canine foul with glittery paints to make some sarcastic comment on the failure of councils to improve the quality of their muck-strewn pavements. Gove, with the twitchy air of a Calvinist minister curtly interrupted midway through a vigorous cloisteral cleanout in the sacristy, told me to excuse him as he'd spotted another batch of truffles unpawed in the corner.

Int: My word.

Man: No, my words. Peering into a plate of peasant's eggs—a slang term for the most inexpensive caviar in the room—was the haunted Victorian hat stand, Jacob Rees-Mogg. This pompous crook was whelped in a family of literal parasites—Mogg's repulsive father wrote the book on "disaster capitalism", i.e. the Christian practice of enriching oneself by predicting the demise of another. I felt the condescension like a sine wave of snooty bile pulsing from his body, coating anyone nearby in a thick patina of terminal smugness.

Int: These attacks are—

Man: Necessary, I agree. I accidentally elbowed the head of mini-Mussolini Priti Patel, the weirdly fascistic product of Ugandan immigrants who fled Imin's tyranny. She had devoted her time as Foreign Secretary to repelling refugees fleeing war by proposing a series of comically sadistic measures that stopped short of harpooning their dinghies herself. Her wet dream was to turn the Kent coast into a Great British concentration camp, where those pesky "economic migrants" trying to enter Britain to undercut British workers in building sites were kept in a state of permanent limbo until the war and famine they'd fled seemed a more palatable option. Her vision was one of a British Normandy, where ack-ack turrets riddled illegal dinghies with bullets, splatting brown babies' brains on camera for rousing footage to accompany the national anthem broadcast every morning. Having elbowed her, I ran speedily to the toilets to bleach my elbow then phone my lawyer.

Int: I'm sure she's lovely with her kids.

Man: I urinated next to Dominic Raab, a fervent hater of human rights more slippery than a buttered eel, and made my way to the balcony where I spotted the blonde Hindenburg himself peering at an owl perched on an oak. "Toot toot," I said, sidling beside. Boris Johnson looked around for security. "I'm a Scottish," I mumbled. I'm embarrassed to admit I completely lost my verbal élan in the face of this Kangchenjunga of bullshit.

Int: Is he as charming as he appears on television?

Man: Do shut your stupid face. At this moment Johnson retrieved his meaty surname from his trousers and treated me to the 1.5 inches of his right honourable member.

Int: It wasn't meaty, big, and bouncy?

Man: Indeed not. "That's a proper English staff. Bet your knavish wriggler merely tapers a summit," he remarked. In a stunned state, I involuntarily shot the peppery lobster canapé I was holding towards his lower half, coating the Boriscock in cracked black corns. My sudden spasm was caused not by the act of exposure—the Prime Minister frequently exposed himself to everyone at opportune moments as a power play—but at the parsnip-shaped weirdness of the penis itself, and the pride he seemed to take in its display. It occurred to me that he probably saw an enormous trunk beneath his legs, in the same way Donald Trump was oblivious to the reality of his mushroom.

Int: That's more horrific than I could have imagined.

Man: Anyway, upon contact, my peppercorns immediately inflamed the tip, causing an immediate rash of ruby-red swelling and acute tip-pain and a howl from the owner. The security detail swooped on me immediately, securing the perimeter around my sternum until I woke on something plastic three days later.

Int: Is that it?

Man: Yes. But in my small way, I had humiliated the Prime Minister by placing his tiny penis in a state of burny ouchness. It's more than anyone will ever achieve at making the shameless, lying weasel experience the most momentary discomfort.

Int: Thank you.

Man: No problem.

5

Interrogator: Please outline the nature of your problem.

Man: I was hired by new TV channel Funky UK to provide pizzazz to their entertainment schedules. My problem was that the two bosses had conflicting visions as to the sort of programming their channel would provide. One wanted to make worthy documentaries on the plight of working families and miniseries on the sweaty travails of warehouse workers, the other knockabout gameshows and reality fluff to appeal to the hard of thinking. "There has to be a way of knitting those two together," the latter said, turning with an over-to-you smile.

Int: And was there?

Man: Absolutely. I devised a show called The Vitals, pitting the poor against one another in wacky contests for food, clothing, and other essentials.

Int: Classy.

Man: In the first round, the contestants' children, who hadn't eaten for days, stood watching as their parents completed a series of physically exhausting and mentally throbbing exercises and quizzes, at the end of which the size of their child's meal was determined. Those in first place received a month of meals for their little darlings, the losers a plate of cold peas for their starving wee nippers.

Int: I assume the viewers sprung up in outrage?

Man: You assume correctly, apart from the fact the very same viewers complaining came to watch the show in their millions. The fight for survival, there's nothing more elementary and exciting for the average viewer. We had many and varied rounds, our most popular probably the one where contestants with disabilities had to answer questions while being bombarded by extreme weather conditions such as tornados, hailstones, and blizzards, the prize being private medical treatment and extra disability money per month. The sight of a paraplegic ex-vet being blown backwards by a studio wind machine, only one question away from the life-altering surgery he desperately needed was one of the most-watched moments in TV history.

Int: Come on. You can't seriously tell me this show was allowed to remain on the air?

Man: You recall when shows aired of people sitting around in rooms having mindless conversations, or when Z-list celebrities noshed wombat placenta for our amusement, the howl of despair that went up in the nation? Then that usual thing happened—time passed—and with it, a quiet acceptance of the new TV reality.

Int: True.

Man: Anyway, our show wasn't too cruel. We always provided the contestants with catering afterwards, plus their travel expenses. We were able to convince the public that these people were heroes to their families. Rather than sitting on their poor backsides freezing and starving and moaning, these enterprising souls had the pluck to fight to feed and clothe their kiddies. Some of them became celebrities who received sponsorship deals and were never plagued by an unpaid electricity bill for the rest of their lives.

Int: Ah, the fastest route out of poverty, debasing oneself on national TV.

Man: Sneer if you must. The ratings speak for themselves.

Int: Presumably the show came to an end?

Man: Yes. We were under pressure to up the ante in each series, and when we introduced a special round called The Saviour, our programme imploded. In this round, the parent of a child needing expensive, life-saving treatment to prevent bodily paralysis and brain damage, was made to complete a sudoku while swerving a series of incoming obstacles such as fluffy tumours, malignant cancer cells swooping from the rafters, and unnervingly realistic fake hearts being lobbed at them by members of the crew. When the contestant fell at the last hurdle, collapsing on his back upon the impact of a tumour, plunging the cash prize back to zero, and condemning the child to his permanent paralytic state, the phones went crazy.

Int: Oh. How odd.

Man: Such was the scandal around that episode, we were forced to pay for the child's surgery in America, and in addition, pay for an expensive LA apartment in which he was to remain until recovery. It nearly bankrupted the company.

Int: What a shame!

Man: Yes, but the child's heart-warming story of overcoming hardship was covered on our replacement show, after which the kid went on to host a showcase for emerging teenage rap artists, popular among the coveted youth demographic. I went from an imminent sacking and industry blacklisting to a 10% salary increase and an extra nine weeks paid holiday.

Int: Landed on your feet.

Man: Indeed.

Int: That's a wrap?

Man: Hey, how'd you know the name of the show?

Int: What?

Man: See ya.

A Fool in the Froth

"Life exists in the universe only because the carbon atom possesses certain exceptional qualities." — James Jeans

I HAVE ALWAYS—or, at least, since I was old enough to take interest in such things—been an avid attendee of the independent coffeehouse. I have never, incidentally, had much interest in coffee as a nourishing caffeinated beverage: I find it far too gloopy for my tastes. No, this interest I declare is more in the nature of an existential voyage into the moodiest realms of the unloved heart, though frothier than that sounds—a dark cappuccino of the soul, if you will.

First, a brief recap.

The coffeehouse boom began in the mid-1990s when the sitcom *Friends* created an illusory line between niche businesses run for profit and expensive loft apartments in Manhattan occupied by beautiful actors with above-average comic timing. We, the impressionable consumers of the post-Gen-X Gen, watched this espressoed merriment and—aspiring to similar lifestyles of sardonic conformity—subliminally OK'ed the international beverage phenomenon that would spawn *Starbucks* and *Costa*, avatars of cosy consumerist excess.

When I first entered a coffeehouse aged twelve, I took against the overpowering stench of cocoa and fag smoke. I thought the adults looked like superannuated twits—well, at that age, I wouldn't have used the word 'superannuated'—but I would have thought them big-time twits. I hated how the fags were perched betwixt their index and middle fingers as they supped down their coffee, nodding at the True and Wise things their interlocutors were saying, and how everyone in there looked worn down by life: cynical and bedraggled.

As I turned eighteen, this was exact reason I frequented coffeehouses. I still loathed the adults, how they held their fags, how they slurped their lattes after multiple cooling blows, but I began to feel part of this renascent coffee-shop counterculture. I felt as though I was clawing closer to some sort of bond with these people so worn down by the impossibly well-cushioned average-to-mid-salaried white-collar lives they were leading—lives so stressful they had to smoke in a distinctly 1950s French manner and chug multiple plastic cylinders of caffeine as though it was an essential balm to their unlimited anxieties.

I also frequented these places as they were an ideal venue in which to affect a uniquely Gallic philosophical *poseur*. At the time, I was pretending to be interested in philosophers, as aspirant semi-intellectual snotbags do at that age, and began formulating an ontological belief system (an explanation to pretend I understood my position and purpose on this planet) centred around the various divisions of society I encountered in coffeehouses.

Based upon thorough assessments of the clientele (staring at people) and measuring in precise detail the kinaesthetic responses to my surroundings (how awkward I felt), I was seeking to identify the precise nature of my being (where I choose to insert myself among the people of the world) and whether the notion of existence was isotropic or anisotropic (whether everyone was the same and not worth bothering about). These factors would form the basis of what was to become my unimpeachable personal philosophy.

I attended numerous coffeehouses when I was studenting. The search for meaning and self-identification (and a half-decent sandwich) began within the first week of term when I was a fresh-faced bundle of nerves, expectations, and academic pretensions.

Undergrad Utopias

Coffeehouses, like revolutions, begin with a naïve, feverish reverie. Among each fresh batch of undergraduates, there are those idealistic entrepreneurs who long to combine artistic freedom with earning a living in the least stressful way possible. So, with their Important Degrees in Textile Design, General Media Thingies, or Advanced Astrophysics with Unapplied Rocket Science, they sublet a basement, and launch their dream like Columbus setting sail for the New World.

I walked in expecting to see students in tweed waistcoats pondering the improper footnotes in a 1946 imprint of a book written by an undiscovered Panamanian genius who slept for nine years in a shed in Tyrol. I was armed with an arsenal of pretentious phrases and glib observational remarks. Instead, I was confronted with a confusing pastiche of the past.

The aesthetic of the place, in terms of the interior design and furniture *Weltanschauung*, was herbaceously echt.* The owners were the spawn of the last great hurrah of the New Age movement: a cult of moneyed beatniks who understood what the words 'ginseng' and 'jojoba' meant. People who festooned walls in patterned flowers and vines to simulate what it might be like to live in a garden centre. The feeling created was one of an indoor '60s Woodstock love-in, minus the free sex, drugs, or terrible music that suggests.

After the first few visits, I began to experience the nausea Jean-Paul Sartre ascribed to the simple burden of having free will.† As I sat on the slim pinewood chair listening to pan pipe renditions of Vivaldi and eating an organic power bar, like Roquentin in Sartre's 1938 novel *La Nausée*,‡ I became aware that not only were inanimate objects and situations utterly indifferent to my existence, but the people were as well.

There were several places I felt content as a human being. This coffeehouse was not even in the running for the top hundred. The clientele consisted largely of freshers from similar New Age backgrounds to the owners—a specimen of human being who up until then remained so alien to me, it was as though I had been dropped birthday-suited into the vestibule of a Victorian estate during a Duchess's debut.§ Yes, the English middle-classes.

Oxford English Dictionary, Various Authors p458, p239 and p383.
†*Being & Nothingness*, J.P. Sartre, p490.
‡*La Nausée*, Jean P. Sartre, p0.
§*The Pocket Book of Incorrect Monarchical Practices*, Bob Jones p290

To my untrained plebeian Scottish ear, these southern English accents had the same whinnying earache quality as a particularly despicable ringtone, much in the same way an English person finds the Scots accent a droning bagpipe shriek of heck. This 'ring-in-itself'*—i.e. the overwhelming alienness of the voice—nagged deep into my reflective consciousness, leading me to the natural result: anxiety and defeat.

I had made a valiant attempt to permeate the fog of studenthood: to extend an olive branch of communication† toward my co-students, but the language barrier, the force-ten gale of foreign phonemes, and the unbearable Muzak therein, cast me back out into the inviolable shade.

When I first went in, I sought to escape my engagement with the world. As it was, being among people who savagely pressed and poked my contempt buttons only served to remind me how impossible it is to ignore the world and its indifference to you. Like Roquentin, I was condemned to be free, forced to mingle with alien beings speaking at ludicrous volumes in the patois of Generation-OMFG‡, and there was *no* escape from this reality.

With this experience behind me, I was on guard as I looked for a more neutral space in which to wax philosophical and be adored. I swallowed my fear and headed for Big Buildings.

Yuppie Yurts

As the multinational coffeehouse franchises forced small businesses to commit commercial hara-kiri, hordes of conscientious caffeine addicts from the city formed resistance groups. Recognising the need to save the start-up coffeehouse from the scourge of universal good service, good coffee, comfort and friendliness, the bankers and whizzkids began to

---

*A pun on the phrase 'thing-in-itself' (i.e. Kant's noumenon—how human understanding is structured by innate classifications the mind uses to make sense of unstructured experience). That explanation, because you can't do a footnote within a footnote, was taken from the *Dundee Encyclopedia of Philosophy*, ed. Mike Wilson, p903.

†*The Little Book of Bad Metaphors*, Danielle Mauve, p280.

‡Contrast with Generation-X earlier for maximum amusement.

congregate in 'offbeat' coffeehouses—low-budget imitators of the multi-nationals.

Me too. It was time to move beyond student alienation into a clearer, more adult form of alienation. When I first entered this genus of coffeehouse, I thought I had stepped into a *Starbucks* in error: the interior design proving that imitation is the sincerest form of plagiarism.

It seemed these places had been designed by an architect who had popped into *Starbucks*, made a few sketches, returned to the building site, then went back to *Starbucks* again to make a few measurements, then returned to the building site again, and so on. An accountant had clearly made a study of which parts of *Starbucks* were helping rake in the largest revenues. It was a disconcerting sight, but at least my cash would be going to ruthless entrepreneurs *manqué*, rather than the established multi-billionaire ruthless entrepreneurs.

Having then been a student for about two months, I began to notice how much pressure money exerted over human behaviour, including my own. One afternoon, sitting among the well-endowed independent financial advisors in their robo-clobber, I began to calculate my own worth in terms of John Maynard Keynes's *consumption function*—an equation which measures your incoming and outcoming expenditure and defines you in terms of what you earn.

Outgoing (£) (per month):
Sandwiches (15)
Rent (100)
Books (20)
Transport (30)
CDs (20)
Grooming (10)
Drinks (30)
Things to Make Me Happier (20)
Chocolate (15)
Miscellany (20)

Incoming (£) (per month):
Job Wages (0)
Inheritance from Rich Cousins (0)
Picking Up Spare Change (0.50)
Being Handed Too Much Change (0.20)
Loan (200)

Being a student supported on loans and living at home meant I had a total income of no pounds and no pence, and a rapidly increasing outgoing total of over two hundred pounds and no pence. I decided to view the world from the perspective of the owners and the clientele. Each person I met had a price tag dangling from their nose, increasing the distance I felt towards my fellow man.

As I sat in the coffeehouse on the replica *Starbucks* chair, eating a replica *Starbucks* muffin, pretending to read philosophy textbooks, I would size up each customer, estimating their net worth in terms of their food, dress, overheard snippets of chat, and compare my net worth to theirs in order to establish a mean value of compatibility. This would determine whether or not we may one day, God willing, be friends.

Using the consumption function, where C = total consumption, c_0 = autonomous consumption (expenditure when income is zero), c_1 = marginal propensity to consume (i.e. how much of £1 you are likely to save, vs. how much you are likely to spend), and Y^d = disposable income, I formulated my net worth. The sum: 346 + −200 − 144.54 = (C) 1.46.

After nineteen years of existence, it was reassuring to know I could value my life at £1.46. My entire being was the same price as nine oranges, or a bottle of supermarket Cola, or a pack of two garlic naan, or a large carton of apple juice, or a packet of Kit-Kats.

Two visits later, I had to leave the coffeehouse. I felt my self-esteem, already in the negative numbers, plunging to an irredeemable value, and the more I gawked at the customers, the more it became apparent they were gawking at me, bringing us to an unspoken mutual agreement that I didn't really belong there. This ontological belief system wasn't quite getting the stimulus it required, and I still hadn't found an acceptable sandwich.

Christian Kibbutzim

Having been spurned by my Anglo-Alien so-called peers and those with a net worth greater than £1.46, I headed for rural woodland areas to, at least, attempt to appreciate in value. Town-wide ramblings led me to the genus of coffeehouse opposite churches erected in the shadow cast by a particularly forbidding redwood. Having been shunned by the trendies, young and middle-aged, I decided this unthreatening direction was what I needed.

I required a kindly Horlicks served by a well-meaning Christian in an Oxfam tracksuit. I had to venture in pursuit of my truth. I imagined I was unhip philosopher Søren Kierkegaard, looking for a mode of life that was true to me—to find the coffeehouse for which I could live or die. In fact, I cranked this conceit up a notch. I imagined I was a biblical figure, perhaps Ecclesiastes' less wise brother Tim, seeking truth amid the silence of the wind.

6:2 And Tim, Ecclesiastes's foolish brother, stepped from the clasp of solitude into a strange and alien place.[1] "What is this strange and alien place," mused he, "where a man can come to eat rock buns with elderly men and women who speak not a word to one another?"[2]

He was a fool.[3] If a wise man refuses to acknowledge the answer when it is sitting right before him, in the guise of flowery tablecloths, beige wallpaper and the disconcerting smell of burnt ashes, then how can he expect to find his own private truth?[4] "I am weak," says he. "I need a sign that this is my truth, O Lord. Is this where I belong?"[5]

He was being a fool again.[6] He was forgetting to take a Kierkegaardian leap of faith: to realise to have faith in a coffeehouse requires one to believe that although the décor might have the personality of a Glenrothes indoor swimming pool,[7] this does not mean he should lose faith in its potential for helping him erect an ontological framework with which to live his life.[8] "But truth is subjectivity, isn't it?" asks he. No, fool, subjectivity is truth.[9]

6:3 Mark eats his bacon sandwich, served by a smiling woman with a pinafore. "This is nice," says he, "though I can't help but feeling the inexorable creep of death in the atmosphere. Perhaps others will turn up soon."[1]

But Mark was a fool.[2] Mark had forgotten the importance of introspection in one's understanding of the world.[3] He was required to get in touch with himself before he could connect with others. "I've had enough of myself already. I want to find other people with whom I can connect in the real world, to stop myself going mad," the fool said.[4]

This time he acknowledged he was being a fool.[5] He felt foolish sitting alone in a deserted coffeehouse with only the occasional bald woman chewing the same cake *ad nauseam*, and a strange bearded gent staring at the back of his head.[6] He began, O vain fool that he was, to find the atmosphere creepy, and was so disturbed that he gave up his pursuit for truth in this particular coffeehouse with haste and little reflection, venturing onto the next.[7]

The bloody fool.[8]

Suitor Shacks

At this stage, a pervading loneliness and an even more pervading depression began to seep into my ontological framework. The outlook so far was bleak. I was alone in a world brimming with potential friends and people with whom I could sulk at bus stops.

Seeking social kinship among bourgeois students, the nouveau riche and Christians was a mistake. Whatever this lifelong philosophical stance was going to be, it would almost certainly involve disdain for these groups. So, returning to people of similar age to me, I ventured into the trendier postmodern coffeehouses—the coffeehouses aware of their status as coffeehouses and what this implied in the global scheme of commerce. This was, I assumed, where the postmodern outcasts— outcasts with a sense of their own status as outcasts and what this implied in the global scheme of social acceptance and popularity—gathered to exchange *bons mots* about the mores of our age.

I was wrong. The people in there were those attractive students universities plaster across their recruitment propaganda: catalogue models with a satchel strap draped over one shoulder, their lips locked in a permanent rictus grin-of-death, as though the Dean of Admissions is behind the camera with a bullwhip in hand in the unlikely event someone accidentally frowned. I never thought these people might *exist*, and here they were, smiling and laughing and discussing the modern music, films and novels I had come to despise.

It was here I began musing on Heidegger's notion of 'being', crucial for our understanding and interpretation of the world. All experience, he wrote, was grounded in care, namely caring for *other* beings. What a curious concept. I might not have cared too much about my own 'being' (although my new mantra was *ich bin mit meinem Dasein zufrieden, ich bin mit meinem Dasein zufrieden*—I am pleased with my existence—but if I could latch onto someone else, I thought, it might imbue my philosophy with a sliver of hope.

To be able to have at least *one* good experience, and to take pleasure from this one good experience, I had to find the being for whom the description 'good experience' might matter (what Heidegger called the existential analytic). So I ventured into the hip coffeehouse, feeling inadequate in the absence of piercing intellectual banter, proper clothes, and any panache with the opposite sex whatsoever. The experience therein, among the minimalist white cubeseats, magnetic tables, and furniture-free feng-shuied floors, was like a series of bad dating ads.

Male, 20. Seeking a woman from whom to derive pleasure so that I might unlock my being in the Heideggerian sense and experience life in richer detail, couching the ontological belief system I have been cultivating in care, and shirking the clueless agnosticism to which I defer on all existential matters. No smokers or Christians.

Male, 20. I am a fun-hating student who pretends to be interested in philosophers, and who lifts random ideas from cumbersome texts and misunderstands how these ideas apply to his own life. I am looking for someone with whom to share muffins and buns, sulk at bus stops, and feel alienated with in a series of coffeehouses.

Male, 25. I am a proper grown-up and everything. My claim to fame is that I once shared a pint with Justin Welch, former drummer for *Elastica*, but that didn't really happen, as it's the standard interesting lie I tell people, as it sounds vaguely plausible and earns me a smattering of hipster cred. I am endlessly sexable. Come to me now.

Despite the powerful attempts I made at establishing eye contact with someone long enough to construct a coherence sentence, let alone a meaningful long-term union, this place was not the venue for finding someone to care about. Heidegger's theory was all very well, but there wasn't a guidebook to which I could defer on finding that one pleasure-deriving source. Onwards.

Frontroom Froth

Well, I didn't so much move onwards on as backtrack . . . back home. A breakthrough in the ontological belief system came when I stopped roaming the streets and set up my own coffeehouse-for-one in my front room. I used the table as a table (replacing the black cloth with a chequered motif), angled a large desk in the background as an imitation counter, and perched a dim 40w lamp at a strategic angle to give the place a last-coffeehouse-on-earth vibe.

I made the decision, based upon the Nietzsche's idea of the Übermensch, to become a reverse overman—I would become the Untermensch—the *under*man. Instead of seeking to advance the next generation of human beings like the comic book hunks on TV's *Heroes*, I would evolve into a new kind of Last Man—someone detached from life to such an extreme as to downgrade a species, perhaps devolving into a form of bonobo-cum-boy, a sophisticated chimp-cum-human with a penchant for sulking at bus stops.

I would conduct this devolution process by blotting out all thoughts of other people and attending solely to basic biological requirements: eating biscuits, drinking cola, and infrequently urinating. I would lock myself into a routine of sitting, eating, and excreting. The philosophy books would be binned, the periods of long pointless thought terminated, and the ontological belief system shattered as I conducted my reverse Darwin experiment.

After an hour sitting at the table with the curtains drawn, the biscuits consumed, and the lamp casting a dim autumnal hue across the beige carpet, boredom soon took hold. If the devolution process was to be successful, I would have to become used to hours and days of near-terminal boredom. I could expect the fur to start growing in thick clumps around the third month, my ears to regress inwards around the first year, gradually morphing into the shrinking hair-covered coconut that would be my head in about sixteen months.

Perhaps I would become the Missing Link, or at least a representation of the half-ape half-human species that evolution wiped out millions of years ago. With this new role, I would be lauded as either the smartest ape or the dumbest man in the universe. Hopefully the former.

I had to, unfortunately, schedule my devolving around lectures and tutorials, and sometimes, instead of devolving in the front room, I would play video games. A much more interactive way to annihilate brain cells. Progress was soon being made—essays were being flunked thanks to the diminishing power of my mind. Plus, my communication was regressing to a series of simian grunts and all-purpose growls and grunts.

This was the solution to my existential problems, the perfect coffeehouse in which to unlock my full potential as a red-arsed man-ape. The only person there was me, which was perfect, as people were too difficult to bother with. The sandwiches were made by me, which was perfect, as I knew what I liked, and there was no coffee on the menu, which was perfect, as coffee is too gloopy for my tastes. The setting was dark, moody, and introspective, which was perfect too, as bright colours would have been blatant self-mockery.

So, with my ontological belief system in delirious tatters, I bolted the doors and began the gradual process of devolving into the Untermensch—the hairiest, smartest ape-man there ever was.

A few weeks into the Untermensch experience I met a woman and began a relationship. The devolution would have to wait. Soon I was frequenting branches of *Starbucks*, guiltlessly slurping lattes, sending texts on my modern phone gizmo, and openly discussing personal grooming habits. The phrase 'ontological belief system' never reared its ugly head again, except when I required an anecdote to illuminate my silliness and increase my naïve charm (which would hopefully prolong the relationship).

It soon became clear that while I was entwined with this woman, who found my torment hilarious, I fit into any seemingly alien social group. With her, the gloomy town-combing exercises became mere ramblings, mere dark cappuccinos of the soul. I needn't strain every sinew to fit in, I gleaned acceptance in the presence of someone devoid of the same self-conscious foibles as me. I didn't even have to pretend to be interested in philosophy anymore, as she wasn't remotely in the inscrutable babble of Heidegger and co.

So, from then on, with the confidence I had stolen from this giggling and lovely normal person, I swaggered into any coffeehouse I wanted, asked for a cup of water, and sat hogging a table with four seats, meeting everyone's eye. To my surprise, most people in there began to look the same as me—lone drinkers in search of their perfect Heideggerian love.

"*Ich bin mit meinem Dasein zufrieden,*" I said into the mirror one morning. And this time I meant it.

The Pomo Martyr

I FIRST ENCOUNTERED Gilbert Adair's work in the former Writers'
Room at Edinburgh Napier University, where I elected to aban-
don a paid career in pursuit of an MA in Unshite Writing. The Evadne
Mount books, proud property of the course organiser and her Thomas
Young power-reader of a husband, sat on the shelves in an enticing hardback trio. At this stage of my reading life, I went into orgasmic spasms
over any book tagged postmodern—i.e. writers writing about writing
in tones of narcissistic self-reference—i.e. the sort of fiction I was peddling in those days (and still struggle to avoid despite habitual dousings
in Victorian opulence or the sentimental hygiene of Waterstones 2-for-
1s[*]). I softly fingered *And Then There Was No One* (not then released
in paperback) and set about fellating the book on a four-hour bus trip
from Edinburgh to Inverness. Alongside that towering masterpiece of
metafiction *Mulligan Stew*,[†] Adair's novel was my introduction to the
kind of witty and candid authorial self-insertion and self-flagellation
that enhances the reader's interest and affection for the author's works.[‡]
This chimed with my fondness for attention-seeking and making a fool
of myself in a comedic way to drum up readerly affection for me through
prose.[§]

---

[*]In Jan 2012, Waterstones dropped their apostrophe (formerly Waterstone's), altering the
name of the firm's original owner to incorporate the spelling mistake. Fictional Adair
defines the difference between bookstores in Switzerland and the UK in *ATTWNO*:
"Your bookshops sell fifty types of books and one type of coffee, while ours sell fifty
types of copy and one type of book." My local branch of Waterstone[']s has no titles by
Adair, except the Perec translation.

[†]Gilbert Sorrentino, Grove Press, 1979. That my first two postmodern crushes were
named Gilbert is a happy coincidence.

[‡]Note from my editor: this pre-supposes an equally self-absorbed reader.

[§]Second note from my editor: otherwise missing in all aspects of Nicholls' life (and for
good reason, which requires no adumbration here).

Adair's final novel is as a fictional literary memoir, written in the arch-affectionate style of his nonfiction, hilariously characterising a variety of literary types, from the wheedling Hugh Spaulding, author of "a cycle of thick-eared thrillers each of which was set in a different sporting milieu," who pesters Adair for ten thousand francs after the failure of *Doctor Zhivago on Ice*; the outrageous egotist and star guest Slavorigin (based on . . . ?), whose collection of ill-timed 9/11 essays *Out of a Clear Blue Sky* launched his reputation as an outspoken anti-American terror; and Meredith van Damarest, "a hellish Hellenist from an obscure Californian college."* The depiction of writers as a gaggle of grotesques holds appeal. I have always viewed writers as the damaged patients in a worldwide therapy group, sharing their manias in the form of stories and novels, hoping and praying for someone to comprehend their pain in between the hourly ingestion of other nutters' fictions. The creative process is nothing more than feverish scribbling in one's padded cell. This notion of writers as far-gone crazies squabbling for love, understanding, and teaching posts in a stifling matrix of insane saboteurs and bile-stirrers was the truth hammered home to me by my MA tutors.[†]

Adair's blend of fiction and self-reference (several characters are named after real people, events and names from his past are scrambled as fiction), alongside his striking finale—the last gasp of a late-period postmodernist—seemed like a devilish and self-replenishing method of telling fiction. The only problem, as the resurrected cut-out Evadne flings at Adair: "Nobody gives two hoots about self-referentiality any longer, just as nobody gives two hoots, or even a single hoot, about you." I had arrived at my literary fascination in its dying or long-dead days, twenty-one years since David Foster Wallace (also recently dead) had attempted to retire the literature of exhaustion with his rambling Barth

---

*My editor and I have debated (heatedly) regarding the existence or otherwise of misogynistic undertones in Adair's writing (present book especially). This being an homage, all negative comments have been struck in favour of propagandist praise.
[†]And, indeed, Martin Amis' funniest novel *The Information*.

homage 'Westward the Course of Empire Takes its Way.'[*] Could a literary movement be considered passé if it never even reached the country in which I was born and raised?

My immersion in the postmodern took me to France and the Americas, where novels are still (according to various undercover sources) being written outside the realist mode with a view to smashing the capitalist superstructure and bringing forth an era of humanist utopia with extra sprinkles and chocolate sauce. I looked in vain for the Scottish metafictionists. I was, of course, already conversant in the oeuvre of Alasdair Gray—*Poor Things*, a Frankenstein pastiche and beautiful marriage of art and text, was required reading at my progressive Catholic school, and the opus *Lanark* with its index of plagiarisms and author-God appearance in the fourth book was an imaginative blast-off into the outer limits of what Scottish people might do with techniques already explored by Queneau, Vonnegut, O'Brien, Sorrentino (two of whom are cited by Gray as plagiarisms). These books aside, Gray's stories and novels are in the fantastical or realist mode—he's a postmodernist whenever it fits the form. This leaves the 1990s novels of Janice Galloway, notably *The Trick is to Keep Breathing*—a dark feminist novel *à la* A.L. Kennedy making use of typographical play *à la* Raymond Federman—and Ali Smith, whose novels are the least Scottish and therefore the most postmodern.

Self-conscious fiction is inherently unScottish. I was surprised to learn Gilbert Adair was a writer *comfortable* with the postmodernist label[†] (not a common position among the Americans, Sorrentino preferred the label "high modernist" as did others). I was not surprised to read that Gilbert Adair was a writer uncomfortable in the Scottish label.[‡] The Scots are a nation of cherub-cheeked teamworkers and camp-

---

[*]In *Girl With Curious Hair*, W.W. Norton, 1989.
[†]See *The Postmodernist Always Rings Twice*, 4th Estate, 1991.
[‡]Adair was raised in Kilmarnock and studied at Edinburgh. He left for France and re-invented himself as an Englishman (with a tinge of Scots). Scots characters appear in his books, such as the housekeeper in *A Closed Book*. It is hard not to speculate on his closed-book childhood. See also his take on Perec's 'I Remember' in *Myths & Memories*.

fire storytellers—the solipsistic and vainglorious are not indigenous traits to this fair land. The commingling of culture, science, and philosophies from other nations is unpatriotic. We have our own thinkers here. We don't need ideas from outside creeping in our cosy idyll when we have David Hume and the miserable internal monologues of J. Kelman for companionship.

This, despite Scotsfolk having a foot in founding the pomo. Walter Scott was among the first to publish under comedic synonyms (Jebediah Cleisbotham, Captain Clutterbuck*) and use the found manuscript frame for his otherwise abysmal historical novels.[†] James Hogg's *The Memoirs and Confessions of a Justified Sinner* also makes use of a spurious editor and found manuscript—a technique later used incessantly by Gray, and in historical novels such as James Robertson's *The Testament of Gideon Mack* (an homage to Hogg). These novels, however, still present provincial concerns. Scottish provincialism has been a problem for Scottish writers looking to explore new forms and challenges without having to bear the burden of Caledonia's past. Their response is usually to flee.

Glaswegian novelist Alexander Trocchi, author of the outsider's classic *Cain's Book*, left for Paris in the 1950s to mingle with the French new novelists and help edit Beckett's *Watt* for Olympia Press, publishing a torrent of grotty and unsexy S&M novels, all written for cash, under that imprint. He moved to Beatland in Manhattan, wrote *Cain's Book*, and downed his pen for the next three decades due to heroin-inflicted impotence. The 1960s British avant-garde scene, populated by B.S. Johnson, Eva Figes, Christine Brooke-Rose (who fled to France in 1968) *et al*, never migrated north. Trocchi's famous spat with Hugh MacDiarmid at the 1961 Edinburgh International Writers' Conference (resuscitated in 2012), where the venerable poet dismissed Trocchi and Burroughs as drugged-up whippersnakes (not that he was *wrong*), highlighted the

---

*Along with Malchi Malagrowther, Crystal Croftangry, Jonas Dryasdust, and, more boringly, Lawrence Templeton.

[†] See *Scott-Land: The Man Who Invented a Nation*, Birlinn Ltd, 2012, for an alternative opinion.

close-mindedness to new forms developed by the postmodernists (an aversion to the young?). It would take Gray's *Lanark* (1981), for some of this creative energy to trickle through the Scots literary landscape (Gray was 47 upon publication).* Even then, the multimedia one-man renaissance Gray was quick to pooh-pooh the label. Rodge Glass, Gray's secretary, recalls in his biography asking if *Lanark* was "a postmodern work, or merely one that has been called postmodern by critics,"† to which Gray replied with a temperamental glower and refusal of a free gin and tonic. Polygon, a defunct Edinburgh publisher,‡ released works from poets-turned-novelists such as Frank Kuppner and Robert Alan Jamieson in the early 1990s, that while "poet's novels," with their focus on lyrical and opaque language, were Calvino-tinged enough for an intrepid or desperate PhD student to rush them inside the Scottish pomo camp.

At any rate, this preamble proves the field was not crowded when I began this fruitless pursuit. I found myself pleased to be a postmodernist (if not pleased to be Scottish). While other deprived terrors from working-class backgrounds sought to become the new Irvine Welsh, clacking out rambling monologues in dialect about snorting speedballs and shagging Sharons and other unhinged yawns of passage, I was working on fictions about M.J. Nicholls persecuting his characters and characters persecuting M.J. Nicholls in a glorious masochistic loop. My characters mocked my Scottishness, teasing me for refusing to take part in the crime fiction *kulturkampf* (Ian Rankin's novels litter used bookshops)§, and snubbing the Scots self-love-a-thon by failing to tip the hat to the Bard (Burns) and the Laird (Scott), and the Other One (Louis Steven-

---

*By Canongate. *Lanark* remains the most ambitious and risky book published by this Edinburgh-based press. Their new fiction output today consists of short works written for younger readers with short attention spans, or books with film tie-in potential. Not an unshrewd business move, only disappointing for pomoheads wanting chocolate novels knitted up as ox skins.
†In fairness to Gray, Glass asked this ingratiating question when serving him in a pub.
‡Now Birlinn Ltd.
§Crime novelists comb the *Edinburgh Evening News* hoping for something scandalous with sufficient plot hooks to turn into gold. Discuss the ethics of this practice.

son). It seemed my acceptance as a postmodernist rested on tossing away the baggage of my Scottishness.

And so Adair, the most prominent Scottish postmodernist whom no one identifies as Scottish, writes his European and deeply English novels, each drip-feeding moments from Adair's past through intertextual winks and private pranks. The results being an exquisite sequence of slyly personal thrillers and pastiches, with Adair doppelgänging Lewis Carroll, J.M. Barrie*, Jean Cocteau, Thomas Mann, and Georges Perec, like a less cracked Peter Sellers slipping on another skin and making magic. I worked my way through the Adair oeuvre, eating up the novellas in a few days, missing the subtleties in the first-person monologues, and decided the best course of action as a postmodernist-in-waiting was to turf the hearth and proceed as an acultural nomad who can write in whatever tradition he damn well pleases (or can convincingly imitate), aware that, at some point, I would have to plunder my Scottish childhood for material. But as a postmodernist, I had no obligation to the truth. I may very well have grown up in the autonomous okrug of Chukotka for all it mattered. It's one and the same.

2

Fast forward several months and I encounter Adair himself at a conference in Edinburgh. The title? The Resurrection of the Author. Guest speakers: Gilbert Adair, Tom McCarthy, Katie McCrum, and David Polmont. I had read Tom McCarthy's *C* with a degree of boredom— Ballardian "death of affect" transposed to a WWI setting was not exhilarating (no doubt I missed the point—Tom writes highbrow lit fic in a post-Derridean mode, whatever that might mean—shall we ask the panel?), and hadn't heard of the other two participants. Katie McCrum was a *Guardian* book critic who had slammed Adair's *And Then There Was No One*, Tom McCarthy's *C*, and David Polmont's *From Juvenal to Jonathan*

---

*A Scot, it's true, but *Peter Pan* is about as Scottish as a pot of Earl Gray in a Kensington Palace hot tub.

Franzen—A Concise History of Postmodern Satire. Polmont was the fore-most writer on postmodernism in the UK, having published *Stop Me if You've Heard This One Before: A Concise History of British Postmodernism* (with a chapter on Trocchi), and *Like Modernism, Only More So: A Block-head's Guide to the Postmodern World.* His books had been roundly crit-icised for their inclusiveness—sitcoms and dense novels were on a par artistically in his universe. Soap operas and sonatas were the same. "Post-modernism freed culture from the chattering classes, creating a world where the lowliest blog could be as brilliant as a Shakespearean sonnet," is an example of his drivel.

Katie McCrum was on the panel as devil's advocate. She had com-pleted a work called *Yeah But No But Yeah But Shut Up*—a scathing as-sault on the exalting of trash that David was proposing in his books. Both of their voices were irritating. David spoke in a sort of laid-back transatlantic drawl like Peter Sellers[*] on 1970s chat shows, a monied affectation that made him sound kitsch and false. Katie spoke like a re-formed ladette unable to shirk her undergraduate inflections—with each sentence, it seemed she was edging nearer an *awesome* or *totes amazing* outburst and squeeing up and down in her plastic chair. Tom and Gilbert were lacking in chemistry, made worse by them being positioned at op-posite ends of the interviewer, Hugh Pegges—a smirking Irish imp with inexhaustible levels of enthusiasm for any words printed on any paper (and the only person man enough to act as arts ambassador for Clack-mannanshire council). The discussion began with the assumption that the author *was* dead in the age of mass communication etc., and how best to resurrect him [*sic*]?

The question was posed to Gilbert. David made a move to speak but stopped himself when he saw Hugh looking at Gilbert. "Well . . . " he replied, taking a moment to reflect. "If the author is really dead, we can reanimate him from the parts of other authors. A limb or two from James, Flaubert, Larkin. We can stitch them together to make a series

---

[*]At the time of writing, I am reading Roger Lewis's 1152-page bio *The Life and Death of Peter Sellers*. Hence the second ref.

of Frankenstein's authors." A slight ripple of laughter for this. Gilbert appeared content with his ripple and the buck passed to David. "If the novel is dead . . . let it die, I say. I mean, us writers, we're like crazed doctors hunched over our manuscripts with defibrillators [defibillayters] screaming 'Live! Liiiive!' What we need to do is euthanise our books." His unfunny outburst made the room uncomfortable, allowing them to forget the lapse in logic that if the author is dead there is no one around to write the dying manuscripts in the first place.

Tom McCarthy went on to speak for a minute about something Derrida said that summed up the topic to a tee and made further discussion irrelevant, however the point sailed over everyone's heads, so Hugh carried on. "I reckon Gilbert is right," Katie said. "Only, writers like Gilbert have been graverobbing authors for most of their careers— pastiches of Mann and whatnot. I reckon it's time to enter the age of the lost masterpiece. I reckon [sic] authors working as a team could recreate the prose style of a James or a Flaubert, using computer technology. We have the means to recreate at the level of syntax the style of these immortal authors—The Greats. Why not work on a sequel to Madame Bovary? Complete Bouvard et Pécuchet? Why do we need new works when we can enhance the canon?" Hugh allowed Gilbert a chance for a riposte. "In the same way we can tell a genuine Picasso from an imitation," he said. "For one thing it would bugger the rare books market." More laughter.

This was an untypical remark from Adair, who seemed to be in a curmudgeonly mood. Perhaps sharing a panel with a reviewer who had shredded his latest novel, a writer who had dismissed Adair's books as "too throwback to be pomo" (David), and another who had never read a word of his (Tom), was a tad irksome. The conversation moved to Barthes's original posit in 'The Death of the Author,' i.e. writer as scriptor, displaced from his text, and Tom spoke about the 1968 essay for five minutes with stops at Lyotard and Baudrillard, which went above everyone's heads (except Adair's). Adair politely kept silent about his 1991 novella named after Barthes's essay, which he expected someone to namedrop, and the conversation took surreal turns with David suggesting authors should be hung up on hooks like meat in slaughterhouses and tortured to encourage them to express their fullest creative potential (no one knew if he was kidding), and Katie suggested all writers become transvestites, with both penises and vaginas, to create a sort of "gender neutral all-inclusive unisex fiction."

The conversation meandered until the Q&A, where things picked up. The first question: "What if I were to tell you right now, you really were all dead?" a rakish man asked, to some nervous laughs. David took a sip from his water as Kate answered. "Do I look like a zombie to you?" she asked, expecting laughs. As she said this, David slid from his chair and collapsed on the floor. We all chortled. "This is the liveliest he's been all night," Hugh said. The panel waited for him to end the ruse, but David was playing dead. Because he was dead. The water had been spiked. Adair crouched down to take David's pulse and a look of horror appeared on his otherwise unflustered features. Pandemonium ensued. The man who had posed the question was seized by the audience and was heard shouting: "I only meant it as a gag! I didn't know, I didn't think . . ." We were instructed to stay put while the medics carted the unfortunate critic to the morgue. The police arrived for the interrogations.

3

— What are you doing at this event?

    — I came to see Gilbert Adair, mainly. And Tom McCarthy.

    — Why?

    — I'm a big fan of Adair's works. I like what McCarthy has to say about fiction even if I didn't like his latest novel.

    — You came to see a novelist you don't like?

    — I disliked *C*, but I like McCarthy's essays.

    — What about the victim, David Polmont?

— I hate to speak ill of the deceased, but I think he's—was—an idiot. His books are apologias for cartoons over novels, music videos over operas. He's popular among the liberal intelligentsia because he absolves them of their guilt for slumming in front of TV sitcoms instead of reading War and Peace.

— What's wrong with watching TV?

— Nothing. Only you can't claim Loose Women* has the same artistic merit as Shakespeare.

— Sounds like snobbery to me. Sounds like you have a chip on your shoulder over this David's opinions. Do you write, Mr. Nicholls?

— Yes.

— What sort of books?

— I know what you're angling at.

— Just answer the question, please.

— Experimental.

— So unpopular, then? The sorts of books no one reads?

— I haven't published most of them, so clearly . . .

— Yes, and don't you think you'd get more readers if you wrote something less snooty, less highfalutin'?

— You sound like my last girlfriend. And my mother.

— Just answer the question.

— Sorry, I don't see what this has to do with the murder of David Polmont.

— Jealousy, Mr. Nicholls. You were so wound up that David had written a popular book promoting the popular literature that you despise, you poisoned his water to exact a public revenge.

— First off, David Polmont is, was, not popular. As I said, he's a hero among a certain group of intellectual slobs who get their rocks off thinking Sonic the Hedgehog is the same as John Milton. Gibberish. No one in the academic world took him seriously. Even lowbrow readers

---

*Interminable daytime gossip show presided over by four loudmouths who exchange mildly salacious banter, sweeping moral judgements on subjects about which they know nowt, and pull mock-earnest expressions whenever required.

took the piss. It was a pose. Secondly, I haven't the faintest inkling how to make a colourless poison, never mind the skill to sneak it undetected in a glass when conference workers are everywhere setting up the room.

— Come off it, Nicholls. It's simple to plot a poisoning. You're the strongest suspect. We've been reading your blog. How do you think this entry, from last year, sounds to us? *Tossers like David Polmont are propagating the belief that picking up the nearest available book with a pastel cover will increase one's intellectual understanding of the world, sensitivity towards others, and ability to empathise, and that the sentimental lyricism of middlebrow drum-bangers like Jhumpa Lahiri or Khaled Hosseini constitutes High Art. Polmont is the sort of pandering populist who was the first to tout reality TV over novels. In his pseudo-scholarly ramble, he defends the copout that in a postmodern world there are no cultural barriers—novels can be about slackers in their pants or viscounts in their pools—unspellchecked drivel from a subliterate teen has as much merit as a polished masterpiece from a genius. Polmont is a first-class buffoon who should be killed with a brick.*

— Clearly kidding from the tone.

— Oh? Then what about this later entry? *I hate David Polmont. His stupid book is going to keep experimental writers out of publishing forever . . . I will never be published because of dickheads like him. I want to stab him in the nose with an ice-pick and hack him to bits with one of those big Japanese swords.*

— I was venting. Clearly kidding again.

— You think a murderous threat is kidding? There are twelve more posts where you state your intention to murder David Polmont. We don't consider this 'kidding' in light of what has happened here. Do you?

— It was unfortunate. But you're wrong.

— Oh?

— Yes. Because it was Adair I intended to kill.

— Was it now?

— You missed the most pertinent detail. Polmont had taken Adair's water by mistake. Adair was too polite to correct him and that's what saved his life. I tried to kill Adair because I wanted to sever the line between fiction and reality in his works entirely. It would be the perfect postmodern murder—slain by a fan at a conference, only a year following the publication of his book where a writer is a slain at a conference. Can you think of a more perfect postmodern send-off? I wanted to make him a pomo martyr! That twerp Polmont had to ruin things with his uncoordinated lunge for the wrong water. Got what he deserved.

— Jones, better call the nut doctor.

4

I was released to private care a few months later, having successfully pleaded insanity. Now a hero in the postmodern community, I received cards of congratulations and hundreds of animated gifs on my Facebook wall. It seemed that my (accidental) murder had precipitated a "renaissance" of the postmodern novel. John Barth sent me a bouquet of hyacinths with a nice card as his backlog was now being purchased in the millions by the residents of Scotland. I published several of my novels with the emerging firm Metabooks who were receiving submissions of novels from fresh-faced writers the nation over. The Scots had "caught" postmodernism at last! Irvine Welsh wrote a novel in which he, Irvine Welsh, remixed *Treasure Island*, only to be haunted by the ghost of R.L. Stevenson who exacted his revenge by remixing *Trainspotting*. A.L. Kennedy wrote a novel about the hellishness of being A.L. Kennedy (unrecognisable from her previous novels, except the protagonist was named A.L. Kennedy). Alasdair Gray sulked, claiming he'd had these ideas first.

Books about books were hip. Kids wore 'I am a character in your novel' T-shirts (with 'And you in mine' on the back). People protested at being considered "people," preferring the term unreliable narrator. Flann O'Brien's *At Swim-Two-Birds* became the ur-text of a generation. School kids took things a step further, living lives as though hopping from one "novel" to another, acknowledging no subjective reality, drifting from scenario to scenario and acting as mere vessels (scriptors) for the texts they produced. A novel comprised of the 444th word of each postmodernist novel published in America between 1960-1980 was a bestseller for two months. Mugs with the slogans 'Eat my performative utterance,' 'Sign my signifier' and 'Deconstruct my deconstructors' were sold in the millions. My own self-published novel *A Postmodern Belch* became a standard on college campuses.

I now had a clear picture of what Scottish postmodernism looked like. Ian Rankin wrote himself into his novel as a rookie detective who outsmarts the ailing Rebus, John Burnside completed an experimental novel on 4,000 beer mats in 4,000 pubs, wherein he imbibed ten pints to create a "fragmented horrologue." James Kelman characters interrupted their usual streams of consciousness to question their purpose in his miserable novels, hopping inside cheerier works like the New Feminist satires of Louise Bagshawe. Alexander McCall Smith began writing literature. When word spread that Gilbert Adair was Scottish his sales also skyrocketed (which pleased me as in his last novel he complained about being out of sight and out of mind—or, at least, Evadne teased him with this truth). I was now in a pomo-saturated Scotland. This, of course, all took place in a novel I was constructing in my head, entitled *My Sad and Implausible Wet Dream*, to be published in my head in a few weeks. I wasn't allowed to leave my straitjacket, so I dribbled the novel across sheets of paper, having bitten my tongue to create red ink.

Writing For Carol

(For Carol)

I COULD WRITE a stunningly realistic story, super-cinematically über-realistic, with characters so real they leap out the page, strangle you, and ride your corpse like a Shetland pony, but I've come to the conclusion I need the validation of women before I write a single word. I must impress a woman, any woman with her wondrously womanly woman parts, with what I have written before it takes on meaning. She needs to be smart, witty, and cool. This isn't some kinky fetish or Oedipal hang-up, Doctor Freud. This is the need to be validated. I want someone to *care* about these lonesome words, sprinting breathlessly across ordered lines, leaping from break to break, making brave bounds into brand new paragraphs. There's nothing harder than writing for your own sake with no readers in sight. I need no approval from men. I have many man friends with manly male parts to sate my social needs. No. I want to see women laugh and puff their lips in surprise and tell me those are some *sweet sweet* sentences there, Chuck. It's not a sex thing. My name isn't Chuck. I have no ambitions to woo women with the quality of my syntax. You think I'm that naïve? I prefer women to men. I write for them. More women per capita read than men. If these words were ever published the chances are more women than men would read them. Let me slap you with more specifics, seeing you look bemused. These women readers needn't fulfil my particular erotic preferences, i.e. they needn't be redheads with cute button noses, polka-dot hairbands, and exquisite potbellies. Discrimination isn't a me thing. You might then ask, is it your intention to impress some octogenarian crone with four warts on her upper lip, alongside the younger, sexier ones? To which I would respond with candour, fine . . . I DO want to impress attractive women. Yes, women with whom I would like to partake in a sexy way. For example, there's this woman I like with longish black hair and short-ish tanned limbs who I have no ambitions to sex as I have never spoken to her (isn't it always the case when you speak to pretty, unattainable women, your sexual fantasies immediately vanish as the sturdy slap of reality meets your dreamy face?) I like her not because her voice has a kooky register, or her views on fracking are screwy, or she has that attitude certain pretty people have that whatever she has to say is the most important part of a discussion, or that she never asks you about your life and only responds when you ask her about hers. Or perhaps those are the *exact* reasons. You'll consider me a masochist, right? Anyway, that's the sort of woman I intend to impress, as incoherent as that sounds. I want no intellectually lopsided women reading my prose. I crave the validation of smart women. It's an inbuilt desire to impress, a caveman tree-swinging look-at-me-Jane thing. I want the person I impress to be of similar smartness to me so their validation means something. Does this make me a chauvinist? Perhaps. Anyway, you are probably wondering, how did I write all *this*? I have pictures on my hard drive of various appealing women and I pretend they are reading this as I type. It's reassuring to have their make-believe validation. Balms the futility.

This brings me to the question of writing for an imagined audience. What if I chose to write for one *specific* woman, like the one mentioned above? Or, more precisely, if I write for the image of one intelligent-and-attractive woman I have never met, imposing my notions of what I think she might like, based entirely on her appearance, onto the prose? How could I possibly know what, say, Carol, this unknown woman with thin, probably dyed, chestnut-brown hair, partly combed over her right eye, mascara running along three quarters of each eyelash, a long chute of a nose and protruding lips (the top lip almost m-shaped) with light red lipstick applied quite thickly, a pale complexion rouged with a little blusher, a teensy divot in her chin, wearing black rap-style togs, would like to read? I can make obvious estimates at her age from the image, but I can't infer anything about her background based on the shot. She is standing before a bland wooden door, but this doesn't reveal much. It is likely she took the photo herself as her arms have been cropped out, one shoulder leaning forward suggesting a camera in hand. The hair arranged over her eye—one strand stretching to rest on her right cheek—seems contrived for the shot. So here we have a woman who likes to take photos of her own face after manipulating her appearance and posts them online. What does this mean? A wannabe model? Vain? Seeking comment from users on her marvellous face? Does she *need* men to tell her how attractive she is for some bland psychological reason, or is she a mere photo-flirt? Does this tell us anything about what she likes to read? Stories that remind her of herself, heroines she can imagine herself into to keep everything about *her*? Is she at that age when people's reactions to her every move is the most important thing to her? Does her face show any particular intelligence that hints at the sort of book she would usually read, if she reads at all, i.e. young adult trash versus serious literary fiction? Carol is my audience for this story. This static image of Carol, whoever she is. I think she would respond to a flawed female heroine, a tad vain but on the case, who reminds her of her strongest qualities—someone whose body she can inhabit, a fantasy self she can use to strengthen her social self and become as adored as she wants to be among her friends. Or men. She's not afraid to read gruesome things but needs redemption or equilibrium restored at the end. So here is my attempt at a brief story, written entirely for the image of 'Carol' with explanatory notes.

Story For Carol

Carol (I use her real name to make clear she *is* the heroine, as invariably I picture Carol's actual phiz when imagining the heroine, as I am writing the story for her, but the character is a legitimate character and not merely a speculation as to whatever I think the real Carol's traits are, although aspects of this speculation will sneak into my depiction of Carol-the-character, as that'd be impossible to avoid) awoke. She stretched her limbs and slunk to the shower (I think Carol would appreciate alliteration—the musicality, the nursery-rhyme bounce of alliterative clauses appeals to those closer to childhood). The telephone

rang as she was soaping and she snatched a towel (as I will obviously picture Carol naked, I allow myself this little peep of breast or buttock—I
know this isn't *for* Carol as such but she would identify with the situation and the presence of my desire would be wrong to omit). Her friend
Christine.

"Hey, are you coming out tonight?" Christine asked. (I want the
dialogue to be as natural as possible without being too stilted).

"Sure. What's the plan?" (This will convey to Carol a sociable, hip
character to whom she can "relate").

"Meet at Barney's at 8, then see what happens?" (Barney's is an
American-sounding name, as I picture Carol as an American kid from
the sass she demonstrates in the photo, although arguably 'Carol' is more
commonly a British name).

"Sure. See you there."

"What are you going to wear?" (This isn't an excuse to imagine Carol
naked again, although the mind instantly pictures a nude body to which
various outfits are modelled and cast off. It is more an attempt at girl-
talk, which is not a strong point in my writing. This isn't because as I
man I can't imagine women engaged in normal conversation, more since
I have no ear for small talk in general, which makes writing unstylised
dialogue a chore).

"Don't know. Something black." (Appealing to the possible semi-
goth side of Carol. This is also the English title of a poetry collection
by French author Jacques Roubaud, with whom this version of Carol
probably isn't familiar, but would certainly eyeball in a bookshop).

"OK, later."

"Later."

Carol arrived at Barney's later that night to find the whole place
deserted. A creaking sound was heard. (Tension and spookiness—up
Carol's street). She called Christine's name then followed the sound to
a cellar behind the bar. (Courageous! Forthright!). The creaking turned
to moans. Moans haunting and distant as though from below ice. She
opened the cellar. (No hesitation, no fear!) Inside, Christine and eleven
of Carol's friends called out: "Surprise!" (OK, so this ending is appalling

. . . I think we have the bones of an idea here, regardless. A plucky heroine embroiled in a series of increasingly scary situations and hoaxes that
lead to genuinely sinister events, and so on until a real murder plot de-
velops. Maybe toss a lover in there too—not so I can see Carol naked
but because Carol is young and naturally sexy, and sex would be on her
agenda).

Something has happened since I wrote that story. I have seen the real-
life Carol on the subway. I'm sure it's her, 95% sure, as I traced the photo
back to its source, a social networking site. She lives in the same town
as me and her photographs show her hanging out in some familiar spots.
This creates a whole new set of complications around my specialised
narrative. The above story was written for the *image* of some Carol I
never expected to see, but I now have the chance to observe the real
Carol as she moves through her life, and tailor my narrative to whatever
little personality traits I manage to spot when following her about town.
This is an exciting development! Imagine the shape my narrative will
take now I know how Carol walks and squawks. I also sent a friend
request to her on the networking site, claiming to know her through a
mutual friend of hers (a gamble, but hopefully she isn't suspicious by
nature).

The world of Carol is wide open to me. Request approved! I pored over
the hundred or so photographs on her profile of Carol in various poses—
she seems more camera shy than I imagined. She is usually the one
behind the camera, taking shots of her friends (mostly well-accoutred
hotties wearing quite fashionable clothes and makeup) and her youngish
parents. She appears to hail from the leafy borough a few streets down
from my flat, an affluent area for professionals, suggesting she still lives
with her parents. In her photos, Carol is relatively extrovert: in bars
she holds beverages aloft and smiles, with her friends she is often seen

with a big beamer on her face. There are occasional shots of her in a park looking pensive or melancholy, with no makeup or attention to her appearance, though she's always wearing trendy, probably expensive outfits. How does this now affect the narrative? Carol is twenty-two—the original photo I used was taken four years ago—the new Carol is more mature, perhaps a postgraduate student or recent graduate. Personal info is scarce. She doesn't update her statuses often enough for me to build a picture of her everyday life. Her statuses are usually addressed to specific friends, asking if people want to meet up, or commenting on the successful milestones of others. She expresses love for her parents and friends publicly, and posts links to videos from contemporary bands, popular stuff mostly. So Carol's character in the narrative will have to undergo a change from a semi-goth late-teenage young woman to post-university woman-of-the-world, someone now grownup and serious about achieving their career aspirations in life. A driven, intelligent, trendy, average graduate girl. What about the real-life Carol (actual name withheld, by the way, for legal reasons), the physical fact of her with whom I was free to contrive an acquaintance?

The chances of bumping into Carol were favourable, having seen her twice on the subway around eight in the morning. I followed her today on the train, where she sat daintily on the seat (clearly practising manners that suggest she's learning to comport herself in a professional setting), wearing a black semi-patterned top and long purple legwarmers. I followed her along the street as she walked—a strident, businesslike swagger, her bag tightly clutched to her hip with a muscular arm. I followed her into a well-known bookshop (no reason to promote them here, the bastards) where she disappeared into a backroom and emerged in staff dress. This revelation exploded my conceptions for the narrative. Does Carol work in a bookshop because she occasionally reads books but mostly likes them as symbols of intelligence or coolness? Does she work there as she is artistic herself, perhaps a writer, and being around books is a natural fit for her as a worker? Does she simply work there as she has retail experience and wanted another position in that field? In terms of the narrative, this takes things up an intellectual notch. Carol might be an advanced reader, she might even be a literature graduate, so my story will have to appeal to her sophisticated tastes or advanced abilities. I return home after watching Carol gracefully putting books away and serving on the till. Observing not stalking.

Story For Carol

Carol arose from her gilt-edged four-poster rococo bed (adding some description here for Carol's more sophisticated tastes, to introduce her to a more ornate prose realm) and stretched her osteofascial compartments, left and right, before advancing to the shower (words 'arose' and 'advancing' here suggest a singular purpose and drive in this Carol). She washed herself with an aromatic ginseng and whortleberry deluxe soap, lathering her skin until her body glowed with the freshness of a new morning (this has the slight feel of a soap commercial, but I want to present a clean and ready version of Carol to Carol).

As she was shampooing her chestnut tresses, the telephone sounded. Expressing dismay at this happenstance, she reached for a silky blue bath towel, swaddling her sylph-like waist. Her breasts, still soapy, felt the cold air of the hallway (not dwelling on her breasts here, but the erotic impulse in me still needs an outlet), her small nipples stiffening in the draught.

"Hello?" she asked.

"Hi there, Carol. This is Christine. I was wondering if you would like to parlay to the wine bar this evening?" (A little more upmarket on the dialogue front for this new Carol).

"That would be lovely, Christine."

"Tonight at eight?"

"Eight is perfect."

"What are you going to wear?"

"I might wear that long black Chanel dress with the Fendi grosgrain bow-pump heels."

"Delicious."

Carol arrived at the wine bar that night to find her acquaintances already immersed in a hermeneutic disassembling of Pessoa's poetics (this is pushing things to the ridiculous, perhaps, but the narrative is shifting towards the hyper-literary, into the realm of ideas not action). She sat down and analysed the fifth stanza of 'O Encoberto' from a feminist existentialist perspective, glossing at length on de Beauvoir's interpolation on Hegelian Otherness in *The Second Sex*. (This version is setting Carol up as a streetwise scholarly adventurer, bludgeoning her friends with her sharp-tongued academic wiles).

I broke the fourth wall and spoke to Carol in the bookshop. Her voice is nothing like I imagined. She spoke with a Dorset dialect, straight outta Yeovil. This ramrods my last version. Our conversation was awkwardly friendly and semi-flirtatious on my side (it's hard to be overly flirtatious when buying the works of Primo Levi, or any holocaust books for that matter). I followed her that night to a local pub, then again another evening to check if she was a regular. She was. I called my friend Tom and we met in the pub, "accidentally" bumping into Carol and her friend Polly. I instructed Tom to pounce on Polly, flirting or insulting her, based how she responded. My hope was that Polly would leave with Tom trailing after her, apologising. Sadly, he overperformed his role, offending both women. I leaned over to Carol and asked her to stay a minute, I had something to tell her. I told her Tom was a recovering schizophrenic. There was mental illness in her family, so this sparked an intimate conversation in a corner booth over a pint of apple cider. I was brilliant. I was sensitive, attentive, an all-round fantastic listener. I avoided everyday topics to protect this intimacy from the moodkillers of weather, hobbies, and so on. By focusing on our families and emotional histories we achieved a closeness that was going to completely change the direction of the narrative.

I met up with Carol several nights in a row and we shared the darkest aspects of our souls. I explained my need to have the validation of women when writing and she volunteered to read something if I liked. This was massive. No longer was I writing for an imagined someone, I was writing for this *actual* someone, whose soul I had tickled for several nights. The problem with the story now is that Carol would recognise any elements I had taken from our conversations for use in the narrative. The last two attempts were something this (actual) Carol might like because she might recognise herself in the narrative, but the new draft faced more complex obstacles. If I included this personal info, Carol might feel her confidence had been abused and stop seeing me. She also wouldn't appreciate reading a transcript of the things she told me filtered through a fictional version of herself. What purpose would that serve? Her problems were not enough to generate a narrative—like most human problems, they had no natural dramatic peaks, merely series of moans and groans. There was the possibility of writing a narrative based around the issues we were discussing but Carol would know it was something I had pinched directly from our chats. If I showed her this document, she would know about the manipulation I had used to meet her, i.e. the stalking. Is there a line between playful pursuance and stalking? It's not like I stood outside her house with binoculars. Last problem: since we avoided boring details about our career histories, I knew nothing about her background I could use practically in a story.

For weeks I held off sharing my work with Carol. We became lovers. Everything spilled out about our pasts. Carol had grown up in Dorset, come here to study anthropology, dropped out because of her mental illness problem, then stayed here to work in a bookshop. She was considering a return to university once she felt balanced enough to study. We were so close, I couldn't keep the secret of how I came to meet her much longer. So, at last, I wrote my first piece of writing directly for Carol, for my audience of one.

Story For Carol

There was once this desperately lonely twit who hoarded pictures of women on his hard drive. This desperately lonely twit desperately wanted someone to love him. He thought by writing great stories he could attract their attention but needed someone to help him through the writing process, so the whole enterprise was essentially useless. Even so, he used these pictures as his fictional muses until he became obsessed with the idea of specialising his narrative for a particular woman until one day he discovered her on the subway.

Because he was romantic and superstitious, he thought 'kismet' (blurgh) had brought them together. He did everything he could to meet this woman and bring her into his life, not caring how crazy he seemed. He had been alone too long to worry about that. So whenever he had the chance to meet her in a social situation he leapt into action and told her everything about his life—everything except the truth about how he came to meet her. When she asked to read one of his stories, he went home and agonised about what to write.

He decided to write the boring unvarnished truth. That he met her through sly, devious means, but now he knows her intimately he's happier than he's ever been, and he's sorry he was so creepy. Loneliness will do anything to alleviate itself. He feels he can write anything now he's met this woman and hopes she will stick around because she feels better for knowing him too.

I handed my story to Carol.

The State of Texas: A Travelogue

I ARRIVED at Houston airport following a stuporous flight from London at nine in the am, UTC. The travelling experience, the usual anting hither and heck to secure spinal caries on benches and thrombosis in long-moaning lines of wait, was ameliorated by the first-class treatment afforded me by my publisher, Strident Arena, who were banking on the success of this travelogue to lift them into debt. I had taken an experimental sooper-soother (sic) medicament recommended me by Dr. Bill Waxter (no relation to my poet friend Mr. Will Baxter, whose raucous verse has never nestled within the warm clam of two paperboards), a practitioner from Austin who co-concocted a new form of chill pill—a sedative retro-sprinkled with lisdexamfetamine to create a tantalising mellow with surprising palatal pips. I was on a two-week trial, having read with interest the doctor's astute piece on the use of remdesivir in halting athlete's foot while bathing in untreated water. This state was perfect for taxiing past the demerara knolls and prominent pylons of Westfield, the cool waft of a spring Texas breeze pleasing the parallel strips of red oak and redbuds, as I hurtled towards the Mountain Goats Motel in Pasadena for a nine-hour recline.

In addition to rescuing the perilous finances of my publisher, I had come to Texas to immerse myself in "the basket case of America" (as opposed to the Midwest, i.e. the breadbasketcase of America) to understand how the average American citizen managed to drag themselves out of bed when around 45% of the population walk around packing heat with no access to mental health professionals and politicians who tell folks to lock and load their cares away. I had no intention to write a winsome frolic on the strange manners of these kook-laced New Worlders, to compose homilies to hominy, paeans to popsicles, or big-ups to barbecue ribs, nor was I interested in rocking up to Trump rallies raising a

quizzical brow to the riotous thickness of the masses, or spending Ther-
ouvian weird weekends with quirk merchants with tragic futures. I had
arranged to speak to several so-called disrupters, the leaders of various
resistance movements bubbling under the surface in Texas. Awaking in
my protocynical motel—the American equivalent of a Travelodge, with
40% more murk—I speedily showered and powered to meet Kay Al-
abaster, the extraordinary woman whose efforts in foetal smuggling I
would experience firsthand in the following text-blocks.

I met Kay, a fiercer incarnation of Holly Hunter in stature and visage, in a verge ten versts from the headquarters of The Society of Liber-
ated Almost-Persons (SLAP), a terrifying dystopian compound located
strategically on the Texas-Louisiana border. Disguised as an Amazon
"fulfilment" centre—an artless rectangular slab of commerce minus the
fusillade of lorries pouring from becalmed loading bays—the compound
had been actioned by Texan senator Broomley Hawkwhip, a furious pro-
tector of the unborn. Inside was an army-style makeshift hospital, where
pregnant women caught trying to leave the state for abortions were held
hostage by ex-military Christian wingnuts with guns trained on their
temples as they passed the time watching TV on a series of shonky beds.
Ever since abortion was made illegal in Texas, neighbouring states had
set up "abortion Ubers", expensive hire cars taking women to clinics for
their procedures and returning them home. Many of the drivers were
nurses earning extra crust after shifts, popular for the aftercare they were
able to provide to the stressed or traumatised patients. Identifying the
common routes to the out-of-state clinics, Hawkwhip had deployed border patrol to catch the offending Ubers, arrest the drivers, and reroute
(kidnap) the women to their "holding centre", where they were held
until the babies were born. Once they'd had their children, the women
were removed from the site and prodded onto the roads with their babies swaddled in a complimentary shawl, where they had to walk home,
hitch a ride, or call a cab if they had the cash.

"They're literally hostaged into having babies they can't or don't
want to raise, and no police force in the state will acknowledge their

plights, all predictably in hock to the whiphand of that shitbird Hawk-whip," Kay explained.

"Today we're freeing several women," she added as we crept half-bent across bone-dry mud towards the least-observed portion of the compound, where a mole in the security detail had been lavishly bribed into helping escort women toward the undergrowth where they could scarper unseen. Crouching by a flimsy bush below a hole in the mesh fence, we kept hush under the friction of cicadas and rumble of the highway, waiting for the bribed mole to observe the torch signal beaming from our torch to his head. Once observed, he returned two flickers to indicate the release was imminent and to ready our legs for scarpering. The situation exploded. Suddenly, three pregnant women were waddle-zooming our way, hurling themselves through the fence and barely stopping for breath as we crouch-sprinted to the escape car and powered off along a series of B-roads and non-roads, avoiding a potential highway ambush in the event of CCTV detection.

The three escapees were harried and sickly-looking women at the upper limit of their termination windows. Kay provided them with water, sandwiches, and warm words of solidarity, spitting venom at the psycho kidnappers while speeding them to their pre-booked appointments at the Sulphur City Abortion Centre, only several hours east. Later I spoke to Kim Schwartz, who had been unable to talk in the back of the land cruiser. She shed light on the stranger things that went on inside the compound. "Our bellies were attached to an ultrasound for an hour every evening. A flock of craven religious nuts would crowd round our beds and fall to their knees before the foetus on the screen before them and say a prayer. They appeared struck with reverent awe for this unformed agglomeration of cells twitchily forming in our bellies."

"These ceremonial hour-long sessions took place across the entirety of each prisoner's pregnancy," she continued, "as part of a Pro-Life package tour arranged by the Fifth Reformist Evangelical Church of the Sacred Jesuits of the Holy Womb of Christ of South Texas, whipping themselves into frenzies of pious fervour at the sight of these foetuses twitching vaguely inside our amniotic sacs, as local pastors performed 2x-speed sermons in babel like glitching auctioneers. When our foetuses shed their cellular state to become born babies, the tours would applaud the empty ultrasounds, thank their hosts, and leave without so much as peeping at the newborn babies wailing in their mothers' arms. In fact, several people requested that the noisy, crying brats were removed so they could soundlessly reflect on the miracle of the foetus on the screen vanishing into life. We were permitted several hours to rest then strongarmed in a state of exhaustion by our captors to the highway outside the compound to commence our motherly duties, assuming we managed to stagger home or hitch a ride. Several mothers, having spiralled into psychosis in their stay, left their babies on the side of the road and wandered into the desert to perish in the hellish Texas heat. The babies, too, were usually left to perish on the roadside, unless a kindly driver came to the rescue. These warped people are more interested in the antenatal and the afterlife than actual life itself. They spend their joyless lives in a state of fury at anyone who wishes to pass their brief time on this planet pursuing anything approximating happiness."

Kay accompanied the women inside the clinic, providing life-saving support as they moved from one trauma to the next. Her rescue package included staying with them at a motel for several days. "It's better they lie low," she said to me, leading the women to their rooms at the Easy Sleep Motel. "News of their escape will be all over social media. People become bored if there is no sighting of the escapees within two days, allowing our women to return home to their normal lives unmolested. We recommend they check regularly for any signs the local militia may be creeping around their homes. Several properties have been firebombed by extremists in the past."

Most women are relieved after their procedures. "Any reluctance we may have felt at having our abortions vanished the minute we were abducted," Kim told me. "Killing a foetus causes these sickos more agony than a mass shooting involving their own kids. To cause these mindless religious thugs acute trauma by taking control of our own bodies is the only crumb of comfort we can take from the whole fucking nightmare." One of the three women I met who wishes to remain anonymous explained that some victims, having birthed their babies under duress, made a point of tracking down the local pastors and placing their unwanted children on their doorsteps. Unfortunately, as a form of revenge, this is useless, as the kids only end up in the local orphanage, a place run by religious zealots. The perfect breeding ground for hard-right nutcases who kidnap women.

Moving on from Kay and the brave women kind enough to share their stories with me, I returned to Texas for a far more terrifying encounter. This involved terrorist troll faction The Libtrigger Boys, whose antics had taken root in Texas two years into Trump's presidency. Taking their lead from their tangerine führer, their MO was to perform illiberal stunts to cause terminal conniptions in the souls of the woke left. They had recently live-streamed a mass school shooting on Facebook in response to recent attempts by Democratic congressman Coky Warden to restrict the sale of Kalashnikovs to the under fives. A banner on their stream read THE 2ND AMENDMENT IS A SACRED RIGHT as the shooters went from class to class executing teachers and children with the perfunctory steeliness of movie assassins. Upon completion of their patriotic massacre, the organiser said to camera: "What you're seeing here is maybe your own kid lying in a pool of blood. Maybe this is your brother or sister. Your response is probably one of horror and repulsion. But you must ask yourself, patriots, what's more important, your right to bear arms and protect our inviolate second amendment, or your child's temporary existence? You can always have more kids, my friends. If we lose our right to bear arms in the United States, that's a precious right we'll never have back. These brave patriots died here today to show you the importance in which we hold the second amendment and that we must sacrifice our lives or other people's lives to protect our freedoms. Whether you're defending your home from intruders, hunting caribou in the wild, or conducting a mass school shooting because mean bitches on TikTok made you feel like a pussy, you should always have the right to feel a cool piece of metal in your hand as a true patriotic American. God bless you, kind folks, and God bless this country."

America's motto is *e pluribus unum* (translated: yesterday's mass school shooting is yesterday's news). The non-stop 24-hour newsgasm of our post-2016 world moves at breakneck speed, from a politician smuggling heroin in his mistress's anus, to a KKK militia furious at liberals who refuse to have a sensible conversation about race in this country, to a multi-state sequence of simultaneous school shootings live-streamed in 4K HD on Facebook. Garnering huge support from Texas lawmakers, The Libtrigger Boys were never prosecuted for their massacres. Even worse, schools started writing to The Boys to request their "gun-ho" appearance at their schools to help with crowd-funding social media campaigns (funds raised sent straight to the NRA), promising kids they too may have the lucky opportunity to spill their blood and innards to protect the 2nd amendment. These live-streamed shootings became commonplace for patriotic headteachers eager to show their allegiance to the stars and stripes. The image of a schoolchild's blasted head with his brain splatted across an American flag became an enduring source of pride for all God-fearing Texan patriots.

I met Sam Trader in a Waco diner. A world-weary, mustachioed park ranger in his late fifties, Sam led a band of well-armed liberals who used the Boys' own philosophy to reduce their spread and influence.

"There are thousands of people in this state who think our children's brains shouldn't be used as propaganda for Trumpian wingnuts," he said, sipping a water. He took long pauses, savouring the relative calm of the moment. He described The Boys' latest wheeze, to force orthodox Muslim women into clearings and have them strip naked. Streaming their tearful undressings on Facebook, the Boys would make "encouraging" comments on their bodies. "American women are proud to show off their legs, their asses, their titties. They don't hide themselves under black robes. The bikini is the official uniform of every woman in this here US of A." They would then proceed to masturbate on the women while praying then release them in their underwear.

"They think it's clever to cause libtard meltdowns, and claim they want to bring about a mass exodus of Democrats," Sam said. "They have a separate mob on the Mexico border, where they set up large trebuchets, placing immigrant families inside and launching them across the country, where they meet their sticky end against rocks. I formed our resistance organisation Men from the Boys in opposition to these psychobozos. They've become a lawless militia in the state backed up by our corrupt cops and politicians, free to execute anyone they feel is against their moronic lib-baiting agenda." Similar second amendment-loving folks who resented their kids being murdered, Men from the Boys took up arms and began hunting down members of the Boys, live-streaming their executions on Facebook.

"The right to bear arms includes the right to seek justice for those who murder our children," Sam said. His implacable logic cemented the group's popularity among grieving parents who had quietly craved revenge for their losses, or those too terrified to speak out against this SSesque militia.

It was tacitly accepted by the monumentally thick Texas law enforcement that if folks were allowed to conduct mass shootings of school children in the name of protecting the second amendment, then it stood to reason that folks could in turn shoot the shooters in the name of the second amendment. I asked Sam if he was worried this logic might result in a stream of revenge killings for revenge killings ad nauseam, but he wasn't worried. "Most folk approve of our executions. We received two hundred superchats on YouTube when we executed the killer of twenty kids at Hubbard Elementary School last week," he said. His dolorous delivery, his yard-long stare, his teary eyes, made me very depressed. I thanked him for his time and headed west of Waco.

My West Texas was a paradise/hell of blood-orange skies over austere curves and peaks, sprawling desert flats bereft of bison or any wildlife, and lonesome highways custom made for Willie Nelson karaoke atrocities. My primary fear was that a mercenary Corvette of hoodlums would rear-end me off-road and perform inventive acts of torture on my eyes in a conveniently adjacent barn. My secondary fear was that a police car stopped me speeding and hauled me over the bumper of my car, blackening my skin with face paint so they could shoot me in the head with impunity. My tertiary fear was that the sun burned a whole in my bumper, setting my engine ablaze, forcing me to stagger through the desert pursued by scorpions and vultures until I accidentally stumbled into a Native-American reservation and was made to apologise for my ancestors introducing Europeans to the Americas in the first place. None of these fears were realised.

I arrived in the desert city of Marfa, an arty haven named after two erotic dramas by Larry Clark, to meet Dr. Bill Waxter. Late for our meeting at the funky Frama coffeehouse, I parlayed with a lawyer for the firm Venn & Penhurst who represented local politicians and broadcasters. He informed me of the trend in American politics to call anyone with whom you disagreed politically a paedophile. This phenomenon started when batty congresswoman Carly Brown Bilge called her competitor in the senate race a "foetus-killing gun-hating paedophile socialist". The technique, in the pre-Trump era, was to accuse your left-wing opponent of loving abortions, of writhing around in pools of aborted foetuses, and to show videos of defenceless (white) suburbanites unable to protect their property from hordes of (black) burglars and rapists. Times had changed, to paraphrase America's bard.

Brown Bilge popularised the tactic of labelling all nemeses paedophiles. An eruption of lawsuits sprung up in the wake of this surge of paedophile accusations from prominent politicians. Newscasters on Fox reported the news in a manner like: "Paedophile Democrat Andrew Yang spoke to a mob of paedophile Democrat supporters in Houston today. This is the second visit by paedophile Presidential Candidate

Yang, and the sixth visit from a paedophile Democrat in the last two weeks. It's important for these paedophile senators to appeal to their paedophile base, while the rest of us hardworking Americans carry on being patriots and not paedophiles and voting Republican."

"These lawsuits are manna for us," this lawyer said. "If we're clever, we can Jarndyce these mothers for years and years, as our opponents tend to produce doctored photos or pay for testimonials attesting to the paedophilic nature of the people they are calling paedophiles. Their technique, I suppose, is to have the word 'paedophile' associated with their enemy for as long as possible regardless of the truth, and more broadly to redefine 'paedophile' as a synonym for liberal or Democrat. The electoral damage is already done, and the accusers are usually elected politicians by the time the lawsuits end and can easily use taxpayers' money to pay their settlements."

"What a country," I said.

"You're very welcome here," he said, skipping to his car.

Dr. Waxler arrived an hour late, a sudden sexual encounter with his secretary Barbara Brockhaus his stated reason. He asked me to refrain from describing his appearance, preferring to remain anon for the nonce.

"She's a cosmo ho," he said, shaking my British mitt.

"I see."

"How'd you find my chill pill?"

"I mellowed pretty sharpish upon popping," I said. "My shanks reclined to an optimum level of cool and I had no paranoid visions of souljacking as the plane taxied to rest in the Houston dusk."

"Yes'm. I've had feederback from folks who said their souls never arose from their bodies into nimbuses of strait."

"You may be on to something."

"Yessir. I want to talk to you today about my new'un. You may've read my astute piece on the use of remdesivir in halting athlete's foot while bathing in untreated water. Well, in the lab last week I magicked aloft twelve particles of that sweet medicine to a new compound, TYP^0. No, that ain't no spelling mistake! Preliminary testing of my new comp revealed that upon taking two puffs an hour, Democrats shed more and moreso of their liberalism and very speedily turned Republican. If I can refine this form-you-lie, you're lookin' at the hottest poh-little-cull proper-tee on the planet here'm," he said, becoming more Texan in syntax as his enthusiasm upped.

"Hmm, I observe flaws in this drug," I said. "If everyone turns Republican, the entire country will be infected with the madness of Texas. Electing untalented carpetbaggers with paltry oratory skills to positions of high office will only lead to the complete unravelling of every institution in the land and a breakdown of order and a swift plunge into a state of lawless chaos where the populace compete to bag the most human kills while nibbling on untasty muskrats."

"Isn't that where we're heading anyway? My drug you could say is an accelerant of the inevitable."

"I wouldn't use that in the advertising."

"Yes. There's also the threat that an imbalance in my compound's fizzies may cause people to politically haemorrhage and vote for the Swan Uppers or the Stalinists. This will require more consideration."

"Thanks for my pills, Doc."

"You're welcome. By the way, watch out for visions of Mary Steenburgen on a plinth. Some users of my chill pill have reported that issue."

"I will."

As I waved howdy-bye to the pretty parchlands of the rural and the sweaty honk of the urban, I reflected upon my experiences with the abortion Ubers, the executors of mass shooters, and the peculiar lawyers and doctors making their plays in the land of plays. It was apparent that America had become intellectually clotted in the faulty vesicle of its own mythology. The spirit of eccentricity that had seen the country bloat phenomenally from the brutality of slavery to the jackhammer pep of modernism, from the illusory convection of creativity and commerce in the booming 1960s to the carefully coordinated creation of a class of superrich autocrats who buy and sell democracy, had long departed. Cutthroat capitalism has turned America into a feudal hellhole, where mindless parasites rally round ultra-rich amoral psychopaths making secret plans to retreat to Mars once the planet they have comprehensively fucked burns to a crispy, cinder-black mass, hoping to osmotically save themselves from violent death by the sheer force of their hero-worship.

The kooky Golden Age eccentricities of the flappers, the rockers, the hippies *et al* have rotted in time and turned poisonous. American eccentricity is now inseparable from political extremism. The kooky is now the KKKooky. As ordinary Americans waved their pompoms for unregulated capitalism, they have seen the triumph of their wonderful country slowly ebbed raw by ruthless, cash-hoovering media moguls, pitting ordinary people against each other every night on national TV by paid hatemongers using their phoney patriotism as an electoral cattleprod. Make America Great is the Five Minutes Hate.

America, a country in freefall.

Americans in America hollering at other Americans in America that they are unamerican traitors to America for making the slightest criticism of anything remotely American. A country utterly unable and unwilling to examine itself. Utterly unable to reconcile itself with its violent and racist past. Utterly unable to temper the philosophy of spectacular greed and lust for power, a nightmare cunningly concealed as a dream. Utterly unwilling to recognise reality. Utterly enmeshed in the decrees of an ancient constitution. Sunk by the veneration of ignorance and idiocy, a country where the thickest loons are rewarded for their thickness, with a public too thick to realise how thick they are for electing thick loons to rule over them. A place of promise, hope, and possibility, reduced to a bleeding haemorrhoid of lying news anchors, lying politicians, lying multimillionaires, with no vision beyond heaping manna upon manna in pursuit of immortality.

A country lorded over by narcissistic billionaires, emotionally bankrupt men who use their vast fortunes not to reshape the planet into a habitable place for the poorest and the neediest, but to construct spaceships to enhance their coolness rating one above Bruce Willis. A country so raped and ruined by greed and self-interest no one can pause for a second without the ravenous hogs of debt, despair, desolation, and dementia chewing them to pieces. A country raving madly in the asylum attic, spooking away the bats. A babbling, incoherent wreck with bloody swastikas carved in its face, squatting on the White House lawn in piss-stained cords hurling turds at the moon.

These were my thoughts as Mary Steenburgen sat unblinking on a plinth several lightyears away, her creepy Botoxed face making my skin crawl. So howdy-bye, America. I hope y'all can afford the therapy.

The Bardo of Abandoned Characters

THE CHARACTER FOND OF EXPLAINING THE SITUATION

H ERE in this bardic space, the sum total of all the world's abandoned characters walk, float, swim, and squawk their way across an infinity of unpublished pages, presenting fragments of their unrealised selves to any passing author who will listen. Fighting bravely to retain their assignation as characters in the vain hope their authors may return to them one day, most characters ultimately morph into new ones, their identities in continual flux, making them unrecognisable to the authors who barely remember the assignation they originally provided for them. As it appears the author of the present work you are reading has cocked his ear in our direction, their voices will be heard for however long the author thinks the reader can stand.

THE (FORMERLY) RADIANT CHARACTER

I wander across a plaza exuding luminescence. I was assigned this designation in a Muriel Spark novelette, long crumpled and pulped sometime in her sleepy '70s phase. So here I am strolling along this plaza, exuding an intangible form of radiance, both literal (radioactive skin as a permanent light source), and characteristic (a peptastic persona where merriness oozes from my every pore), respecting both radiant interpretations, blinding other characters with my wattage while bombarding them with upbeat pith in imitation of Dame Muriel. "WHAT A LUVVERLY DAY!" I say to them as they run to safety, shielding their peepers from my floodlight lumens. The impossibility of making friends in person or online (my radiance made focusing on a laptop screen impossible) meant I set up in business as a rent-a-lamp, providing free illumination for sporting events and the stage, taking what pleasure I could in the brief orders I received from lighting directors to stand in a certain position and move to the left an inch and so on. Ultimately, my excessively luminous personality was not able to cope with this fun-free servitude, so I had no choice except to puncture my skin until the lumens dimmed. My body, at the end of this pain-packed self-mutilation session, was a siege of scars with flickers of light coming from unbowed pores like a series of pocket torches with batteries expiring. The havoc wreaked on my figure smashed my self-confidence, my remaining in any way radiant an impossibility, leaving me no choice except to pass from my assignation the way a Volkswagen Golf moves along a B-road at four in the afternoon observed by precisely no one.

THE SELF-SATIRISING CHARACTER

I hit the streets in a pair of comical brogues, blue-tipped and red-heeled, taking a satirical swipe at the extravagant footwear I was prone to wear. I pointed out to several onlookers the shoe choice, expecting them to remark on the chucklesome nature of my pedal palette. "You'll note the garish colour scheme at the tip and heel," I said, helping them glean the subtlety of my self-satire. "I've never seen you before in my life," one of them said. "Rest assured that the choice of colours on these shoes serves up a humorous self-slap to my notoriously fashion-free sense of footwear!" I said. They had no idea that I was actually satirising a satirist trying desperately to satirise himself, taking my satire to whole 'nother pleasingly recursive level of cleverness.

THE CHARACTER WHO INVENTS VEGAN BANDS

Tootling along the lakeside, I had a moment's inspiration! The Cumin League. Tofu Fighters. Bread Zeppelin. Nick Kale & the Good Seeds. Soy George. Half Man Half Biscoff. The Shaming Lips. Big Star Anise. The Mango-Betweens. If you have any more, please write to me.

THE CHARACTER MAKING EXCUSES FOR NOT READING YOUR QUARTERLY

I have been unable to subscribe to your lateral literary fascicle for the last two issues for very heavy agricultural reasons. Namely, pak choi winded me in the autumn. Taproot mould—a charred mushy taint six centimetres down, inviting to malign invertebrate nibblers—savaged seven hectares of my turnips, eclipsing the Portsmouth Rot of 1978 that commenced the craze for cheaply tossed Chinese cabbage, flooding the market with a sickly fungible exotic spiciness irresistible to the English palate. The steady harrumphing in agribusiness following Brexit's public capture had kneaded a sense of warm complacency into the largely cretinous minds of turnip traders, causing us to lean on our laurels and hardy ways to weather any hypothetical storms . . . thus utterly unprepared for this heinous taproot assault.

I had always sneered at rivals recruiting taproot monitors (burly Mongolians on hand to ensure a virile cultivar length, to hunt and kill any hairy-backed nibblers nesting in the radicles, to keep the layers of grot to a washable minimum) to sentry their cabbage progress. Those farmers who employed these strapping farmhands to farmhandle their mouldering roots swerved the pak choi pounding (from Vietnam, this time) and continue to pay their dues to the Conversative Party as the rest of us pack our kitbags for the city. Soon my farm folded with the retractable snap of a multiplex chair. This is why I would advise your rustic readers to consider the wisdom of investing in an experienced vegetable watcher from a landlocked socialist republic. You cannot predict the evils that lurk there under the loam, and you cannot trust Mother Nature not to poison your lot with sudden upturns in soil moisture.

You may therefore appreciate my short-term exclusion from your literary orbit and excuse the pungency of my neglect.

THE COVIDIOT CORRECTOR CHARACTER

As you're sweet enough to observe me, let me explain my origins. I was working as a doctor in a ward populated by paranoid anti-vaxxers and one morning I chose to amuse myself. My patient was wearing a flowery tabard and the expression of a half-witted nincompoop (a redundancy, perhaps, but it paints a cruelly accurate picture). I spoke into her open mouth the following eminently sackable words: "First, the syringe is peppered with the foetal tissue of freshly murdered babies." Then I said: "Next, twelve aborted foetuses are put in a very big blender and frothed up into a foetal milkshake. This is combined with proteins scraped from the perineum of Mexicans, Democrats, and Muslims, and tweezered into the vaccine." "I knew it!" she screeched. The following morning I awoke to a barrage of placard-waving no-vax numpties outside my house, including one man dressed as a hypodermic needle, who followed me to my car clutching a foetus doll screaming something about the blood of orcs. At work, I was shoved into a meeting with the practice manager, who told me that in the event of the media pressure, and my failure to make a sarcasm-free apology, I would be reading my P45 rather than Paula Hawkins on the train home. The next morning I received a direct message from an anon asking me to hook up with him on Discord. An hour later, I met him on a pavement near some clumps of hay. He introduced himself as the leader of an organisation known as The Correctives, named after the novel by Georgie Franken. They were paid by concerned individuals to vaccinate "vaccine sceptics" who refused to have a vaccine for various stupid reasons. They were part of a movement looking to "mop up" the detritus of the world, starting with the public assassination of Tucker Carlson. When they murdered Tucker Carlson in front of his wife and children on national TV, they believed they would herald the start of a new system featuring a substantially diminished level of chaos and insanity. I started work Wednesday.

THE CHARACTER WITH A TERRIBLE IDEA EN ROUTE TO A FUNERAL

I was on my way to bury my mother when I had the following idea for a story: Harlan Coben was an immigrant from Aleppo whose entire family had perished in the chemical assault from Al-Assad and Putin's brutal military assault, blinding his children with toxic sulphur before succumbing to their fatal burns. He had been in another part of the city retrieving limbs from the remnants of broken buildings at the time, then spent three days trying to retrieve the chemically desiccated remains of his children and wife from the rubble. Numb with horror, he made the decision to leave the country to pursue a life of vice and chaos in Europe. Unfortunately, the immigrant perished in the English Channel en route to Britain. He set off on the perilous boat crossing believing that Allah would see his pass safely, that Allah's will in killing in his entire family was something to be respected, that Allah would provide him with hope and a future, that Allah would reunite him with his family in the afterlife. But as the vessel started to sink, he wondered if everything he believed his entire life was a total lie, everything a false hope, and whether relinquishing his false beliefs might somehow provide a real redemption and comfort, or if there's no such thing as redemption or comfort at all. I was on my way to funeral when I had this idea for a story, and by the time I left the funeral, I embarrassedly banished the awful idea to the recycle bin of my mind's hard drive.

THE CHARACTER EXHILIRATED BY A CHILD BEING CRUSHED UNDER A PARSNIP LORRY

As the rain piddled upon the hair of a boring redhead named Christine— that's me—a cargo lorry carrying four hundred parsnips careered into a wall, flattening a passing toddler. I was shoving my pregnant ass up a pavement towards the bookshop to footle through the begrimed paper-backs of yesteryore and witnessed the accident. The lorry—a commercial vehicle bloated with parsnips—startled at the sudden onset of rain and the presence of me leaping across the road in my pleats, swerved towards the toddler, some seven steps ahead of his momma, and ploughed into his hairless torso at 39MPH, flattening him beneath the brutally thick wheels of the commercial vehicle. On the nearby pavements, the public made a collective moaning sound somewhere between sorrow and barely restrained excitement, unsheathing their phones for immoral paps and resheathing them in shame as the toddler's corpse was tagged and bagged by the police several minutes later, and the mother expressed her sorrow in a series of long shrieks lasting a week-long ten seconds. Forty-nine minutes after impact, the road was clear, and I was nudged back into the norm.

"I saw a toddler crushed under the wheels of a parsnip lorry," I said to Alfie, the owner of the shop of books.

"That the beginning of a folk song?"

"No, I actually witnessed a toddler's slaughter under the wheels of a lorry."

"Grim."

"The weird thing was . . . I found the thing exhilarating."

"Yes?"

"I felt no sorrow for the loss of life. I thought that this was an exceptionally exciting thing to happen to me on the morning walk, and that the death of this toddler was worth it for the temporary pleasure I felt in the slight deviation from the norm."

"That is normal. You had nothing invested in that toddler and the adrenaline kick that kicked in was of more use to you than that toddler's future."

"I am pregnant. This does not bode well for the future of the sprog inside me."

"Wouldn't sweat it much."

"I actually feel like laughing."

"Why not?"

I started with guilty titters that sharply intensified into bone-shoogling haw-haws of the most outrageous nature, thumping the table and avalanching a stack of Updikes, until my legs and feet were sodden with wee.

THE CHARACTER STUNNED BY THE USE OF CIRTUS FRUIT IN EROTIC ANTIWAR PROTEST

Opaline peasant moon waxing on the hot mulch of the Republic. Broad-chinned salter of snails Komma Drama skirting the oddness of the perimeter as thimbles of tuica burn the throats of the spent humbles. "This one concerns the vast indignance of sour things," the narrator says, in an inkling. Approaching the nine-by-ninety-nine-sized shed of Draga Driscoll and her operation, Komma observes a series of sounds, from the gasp accompanying the withdrawal of a hand hotly caught on the sim-mer of a stove, the shudderous moan as a series of turds escape the body, and the stunned slump as a man vaults the cliff on a microlight.

Inside, a fat-lipped tinker woman, her hips two meaty bothers, was rotating a half-lemon around the erect penis of a wincing man. She squeezed the remaining drops over the plank of his stiffness and ran her tongue along the length, sourness implicit in her face. Over there, a woman was feeding lemon halves into the mouth of a man she was furiously masturbating while below another was mashing lemon against his pendulous testicles. Sally Drinca, who worked in the hardware store, was lying naked in pool of lemon rinds while one man squeezed juice into her eyes and another penetrated her with his surprisingly taut penis. Her screeches from the pain of the lemon intersected with the clitoral pleasure in a sound that resembled a banshee sucking the venom from a puff adder.

A long, broad-shouldered man with a large moustache rubbed a lemon along the open vagina of a woman who was tonguing the anus of a stocky man having lemon juice squirted into an open wound he had created earlier with a knife.

"We victims of the Cartonnage Uprising come here today to explore the limits of the sweet and the sour. These lemons are instruments of war, calibrated to destroy the plush fabrics of our republic, while our bodies are instruments of revolution. Here we bring together the elements in a tortured admix to prove that the instruments of revolution will triumph over the sour torments of war."

After she finished, a man inserted a lemon slice into her anus, while another penetrated her with a lemony penis. The sounds were not reassuring.

THE CHARACTER RECALLING THE TIME HE LOST SOMETHING FROM THE POCKET OF A MAUVE CAGOULE

I was walking along the pavement when I recalled the time I lost something from the pocket of a mauve cagoule. I recalled the time when something fell from the left or right pocket of the cagoule and landed on the pavement with either a thud or a thump. I recalled that moment with astonishing clarity—the near-sensual kinesis between my hand and the item, the scent of whelks and vaseline in the air, the hum of local choral singers—and I smiled at the recall of that lovely kinesis, although I could not remember what the item was, and wondered if the item might have been something of import, like a bank card or a photograph of a loved one, perhaps a mother or a gerbil. The prospect of such light and unweighty items thudding or thumping on a pavement was improbable, so I concluded that this item must have been something more substantial, such as a crystal ball or a hardback novel. The prospect of a crystal ball or a hardback novel fitting into a left or right pocket of a cagoule was improbable. The thought that an item of sufficient weightiness might fit into a small pocket was unlikely, and then I recalled how a paperweight might fit inside a pocket, and that a paperweight, if it landed on the underside, might make a thudding or a thumping sound (although a paperweight was more inclined to land glass-side up, and smash or crack or clunk). I had never had occasion to use a paperweight across the short lifespan that Yahweh has allotted me, so I considered other possibilities.

I considered a tub of something, such as a tub of eczema cream, then I recalled that I am not a sufferer of that particular skin condition, so I parked that notion. I recalled that I am however a sufferer of psoriasis, and that I might have been walking around with a tub of psoriasis cream, and that it was possible that I had placed a tub of that particular cream into the pocket of this mauve cagoule, and that the tub had emerged from the pocket with a thud or a thump. I took my penis in hand as I recalled this incident.

THE CHARACTER WHO BEDDED KEITH RICHARDS FOR THE NOBLEST OF REASONS

I stepped from the ruins of the old cathedral where a F-34 missile had blown apart two thousand years of history, vowing that I would marry Keith Richards. My father was an enthusiast of American rock music, in particular the songs of The Rolling Stones, who were known as outlaws and libertines. I had listened to a song with the lines 'I see a red door and I want it painted black' and thought about the infidels who were trying to destroy my country, and the song always made me cry. I soon realised that The Rolling Stones were in fact not outlaws, but rich libertines, and I contrived a plan to help rebuild my small nation from the rubble caused by our enemies.

I had read in the American media about Keith Richards's fondness for young wives, and that he had recently divorced from his twenty-three-year old bride, whom he had married six years ago, when she was only seventeen. I had turned fifteen the previous year and was picking up comments from the menfolk about my beauty, so I asked my mother if I might move to America with the intention to marry Mr. Richards and use his funds to rebuild my country. My mother approved of this plan. I practised the application of kohl to emphasise my striking wild Eastern eyes, and the use of make-up and lip gloss to make my features more like the pouting American models.

Six months later, I had enough money for a one-way flight to Los Angeles. I had researched the names of modelling agencies in that country, and found a company called Gruber & Gruver who had also taken publicity photos of The Rolling Stones. I moved into a small motel room and a few days later, went to the agency to present a photograph of myself. Fortunately, my natural beauty and striking Eastern appearance was noticed by a senior employee at the agency, and I was taken into a room for my first photo shoot. I posed in all manner of photographs, most tasteful, but in several I was required to cover my breasts with my hands. Although I felt shame at these actions, it seemed small in comparison to raising my beautiful city from the ashes.

To make conversation, I asked if the photographer knew The Rolling Stones, and fortunately, they were due to appear next week for a new photo shoot. As an illegal alien in the country, I would not be paid until my documents were shown to the company, so I nervously retreated to my motel room for the week, passing the time watching television and dreaming of my homeland.

The week rolled around, and I showed up at the agency for a shoot, hoping to catch the eye of the Rolling Stones. Preoccupied with their own shoot, my photos had already been taken when they were with another photographer, so I hung around hoping to catch the eye of Keith Richards. As the rules were lax for models, I caught Bill Wyman's eye before being escorted from the building. Bill pointed me out to the other men for ogling. I caught Keith's eye and smiled. From that moment, I had Keith in my clutches.

A series of dates followed, and Keith politely waited until I was sixteen before taking my virginity. Although I found the ageing flesh repulsive, I yielded in the hope of inheriting his fortune, or convincing him to help rebuild my city. Sympathetic, Keith decided that the Stones would perform a concert in aid of my country. This was not enough. I required all his funds. This brings our story up to date. As of now, I lie in bed in splendour behind the kind-hearted Keith dreaming of my village, knowing in my heart that I wish this man to die so that I might return to repair it to its former glory. I am thinking in the meantime of setting my family up in a house here, while I wait for things to settle.

THE CHARACTER WHO DROPPED A USB STICK IN HIS FATHER'S ASHES

My father was—

Hmm. Perhaps not. Does the world need another description of a man's father? Consider the number of fathers hewn in print, from the first father, God in Heaven, YHVH Himself, in that smash bestseller *The Bible*, to the more recent fathers like Walter White from *Breaking Bad*. The father has been penned to perfection in literature. There's the faultless crusader for justice, Atticus Finch, the father living through his children, Pere Goriot, the father pinballing his childrens' affections, King Lear, the quintessential drunk deadbeat dad, Papa Finn, the creep of a stepfather, Humbert Humbert, the father who auctions his children, Michael Henchard, the quiet loving father, Mr Bennet, the hopeless pauper with a Heart of Gold, Bob Crachit, the right-wing philandering prick, Rabbit Angstrom, the grandiose patriarch-of-old, Big Daddy, the father who resents his daughter having rights, Mr. Stanley. In television, there's the proud Texan keeping-it-real, Hank Hill, the loveable yet harsh patriarch Dr. Heathcliff Huxtable, the murdering lunatic with a winning smile, Tony Soprano, the neurotic Frank Costanza, the revolting lecherous rag-and-bone man, Alfred Steptoe, the racist xenophobe, Alf Garnett, and the father that named his son Fernando, Alan Partridge.

For the sake of shorthand, my father was a cross between Hank Hill and Rabbit Angstrom.

Either way, he's dead.

And I dropped a widget in his ashes.

The widget was a small USB stick, and USB stands for Universal Serial Bus. The word 'bus' in this abbreviation is strange. Bus is a blanket computing term for something that transfers data whether from computer to computer, or within a computer, and includes optical wires, USBs, internal data parts like motherboards, and external ones, like connections to a printer.

On that USB?

Several volumes of autobiographical writing. The sort of stuff that never came up in father-son chats. The first volume, entitled *The Steve Albini Papers*, chronicled in precise detail the unkind fantasies and feelings that burst forth while listening to the recordings of Steve Albini's various musical incarnations. You understand that retrieving that USB was a choice I had to think on with care. This was not the sort of man you sat across from in bistros eating sachertorte, or the man with whom you exchanged remarks on the tortuousness of the latest Liberal Democrat leader. Like a pebble-dashed Ballard, I had a father in hock to some kind of PTSD, a father who vented his black fantasies through the medium of the Steve Albini oeuvre.

So, for now, the USB remains.

THE CHARACTER WHO STAGED A SPONTANEOUS ORGY IN REVENGE FOR AN UNWANTED ICE RINK SURROUNDING AN UNFAIRLY NEGLECTED HISTORICAL MONUMENT

The Krumpli Temple of Lepers had sloughed into insolvency when the council contrived the wizard wheeze of encircling the ancient monument with a skating rink for kiddies and thickies. I was managing the Temple when praise for the farcical suggestion erupted on social media. It seemed the local village was more interested in powering across artificial ice on skates than exploring an airless cubic foot of medieval carvings of men with their limbs hanging off. Who'd have thought? Having burned my eyes beyond repair with the public's inanity, I stoically waited for construction to begin.

A year later, with the skating rink curling in blight round the Temple, having lunged passionately into my newly minted pastime of chronic alcohol abuse, I wandered half-cut around the rink and capsized backwards on my flabby middle-aged arse, splaying my legs and spraying expletives into the bitter evening. A stockily proportioned young hunk helped me to my feet.

"I fell on my backside," I said.

"I noticed. Here, let me help you," he said.

He was a broad-shouldered youth with the cowed appearance of a severely whipped Slav. He took my hand and tugged me to safety, liberally stroking my hot palm in an unmistakable ruse to conquest. I thanked him with a milkshake and ranted to him about the Temple, which he asked to see, if only to shut me up. Inside, I stood on a plinth and licked his left cheek. I ran my tongue around those fulsome Slavic lips until I prised the man from the boy. He retaliated with a powerful tongue-thrust between my lips, seizing my waist for a full minute of hot necking. I ran my tongue along the sinews in his thick neck, roughly nibbling on his chin as I lost control of my urges.

It had been twelve years since my last spontaneous shag with a stranger. The encounter had left me with the idea for a splendid scheme to attract people to the Temple and stick one in the eye of the ice skaters.

The week after, I invited ten flabby-arsed middle-aged women to the temple alongside an equal number of 16+ teenagers who I lured with promises of free beef. As the teens entered they viewed a seraglio of lurid satin where naked elders sat on mattresses waiting to taste their nubile cocks. Sashaying up to the boys, violently thrusting their trousers down and taking their meaty members in their mouths, the spirit of depravity seized the stunned youths, and soon the women rode their exalted bodies like rodeo queens, pelvically milking the semen from their bulging sacs until it poured forth in a summer harvest, coating the tongues, breasts, and cunts of my fellow lusty wenches.

My spontaneous orgy lasted the whole weekend until the young boys' sacs had completely shrivelled inside their perinea, rendering them completely impotent for weeks to come. Once returned to the community, the young men went out of their way to avoid the young girls courting their attentions, furtively sneaking to the poolhalls until their libidos made a tentative recovery. Thus began a lucrative racket at the Temple. By charging an entry fee per orgy, we made more in a month than the Temple made in two years, and ran rings of profit round the ice rink, hastening its demise.

THE CHARACTER WHO IS A BAD MAN

I consider myself a bad man. An example of why, you seek? Here's one. This old man stumbled from the Squatter's Arms, his moth-eaten flannel trousers caked in mud. His long unkempt beard had become caught in the zipper of his beer-sodden raincoat. As he attempted to walk in a straight line along the pavement, thrusting each barely compliant leg forward in a poor approximation of linearity, he felt the tugging sensation in his chin more acutely. He stopped and released a loud moan, pulling his beard harshly, trying to separate the hairs from the unyielding mechanism of his zip. As two children looked on, the bearded man attempted to maintain a façade of being a kindly and loving uncle and retrieved from his pocket a packet of mints. In his own beery eyes, he was like a cuddly grandfather offering his beloved daughter-in-law a sweet, but to the child's horror he proffered a palmful of sick. This observation should tell me something about the human condition. It should prove to me that even the world's most lost souls are capable of redemptive acts of misplaced kindness. Instead, my pleasure at the horror of this child and the anecdotal version of this I would relate later made me explode with happiness. You see? I am a bad man. There's no doubt.

THE CHARACTER WHO REVIEWS HIS DREAMS

I was wandering pantless along a silken pavement humming piano melodies from the first Silver Mt. Zion Orchestra album. A headless woman with the stump-like legs of Diana Forester approached and whispered something momentous to me, and the scene shifted to a knoll somewhere in Montenegro, where a frog chorus ribbited out Wham's

'D.H.S.S Rap', their leader sprouting the head of George Michael. I approached the frog Michael and asked him what the secret of love wasn't. He smirked at me in a manner frightening and burst into flames. The frog chorus followed, and a series of shrill ribbit-shrieks forced me to awake, at 3.56AM, to appraise the substance of the dream.

Overall, I was impressed. I consulted my DREAM REVIEWS ringbinder and looked over the last several. A robot holding a Victoria sponge pogoing around my childhood bedroom. The last whatsapp I had with Diana before The Great Thaw, broadcast on billboards across the entire state of Idaho. A childhood cat sprawled across the bedroom carpet as a miniature Shania Twain sang her one famous song on the curve of his hairy sac. These were interesting dreams in terms of their inventiveness and captivatingness, although it was rare these progressed into narratives with their own amusing or horrific twists. The rating: Inventiveness . . . 8/10, Excitement . . . 8/10, Surprisingness . . . 9/10, Insight into Psyche . . . 4/10.

THE CHARACTER WHO LEFT

Tweezered betwixt the phalanges of a human threat, the pool of mould twitched inside the egg. Mould in a Moebius round the circumference, the implication of a crack in the fragility of the shell's hollow. The human threat brought the egg closer to a squint of light in the brickwork to reveal a scaly prawn-like curl bedded in its own blood. Fear shot the egg from the threat's hands against the hard brick. The egg split against the wall, where a creature slid from the shell to a pile of embers from a faded memory of fires.

The creature, unborn, liquesced in the fluid, until a very sharp burp brought the small thing's heart to life. A small sharp calliper sprung from its sinewy spine, slowly extending like the antennae of a black widow spider. The scaly body swiftly sprouted tufts of slate-grey fur, upfurling across the curved spine. Soon, a second calliper sprouted and the creature inched across the embers like a drunk peanut, moving through the room towards the foot of the human threat who sat with a pipe reading an almanack.

Extending a calliper, the creature pierced the shin of the threat, transferring the rheumy poison nestling in its cloaca into the man's blood. In an hour's time, the human threat walked from the cottage to the town towards the local school. Tempting the children with a roll of Hungarian chocolate, he took the assembled into a small wormwood hut. He bolted the door closed and surrounded the roof in twine. Next, he lit a fire. The next morning twelve children's remains were found charred inside the shed.

The man returned home to urinate and observed a blood streaming from his penis. Sweat poured from his arms. It became apparent that the man was leaking from the inside out. When the police officers arrived, the man had expired all fluid from his pores, and was little more than a shrivelled husk on the stone floor.

That man was my father. It was for this reason, along with the unfair persecution of actuaries, that I left the village of Paradicsöm.

THE CHARACTER CAUGHT IN AN UNDEFINED PROTEST

I was caught up in a political protest. The placards and banners being thrust into the air in the hands of these vociferous and vicious protestors read "we want change", and in an act of mischievous satire, I reached into a coat pocket to retrieve a 5p piece to hand to one of the protestors, before thinking twice about upsetting them and meeting their wrath, for one or two of them had been quite violent in their shouts and thrustings of the placards, suggesting that a wrong word said might result in a similar thrusting, except with a fist into a face, that was mine. I also had no 5p in the cagoule pocket with which to make this satirical riposte to their placards, so I approached a small woman with less vengeance in her face to ask her what sort of change the political protestors were seeking to enact with their placards, and the small woman said that she was unsure, and that I should ask one of the more senior protestors if I wanted more specific information about the nature of the change for which the protestors were protesting. I approached a tall man whose vehemence levels seemed less menacing than some of the brawnier, tattooed bawlers nearer the police officers who were holding riot shields and truncheons, and asked him what sort change the protestors wished to enact with their placards and banners. The man accused me of asking the wrong sort of question and misrepresenting their cause with such a stupid enquiry, and that I should stop being an enemy of their cause, and come with them, and that if I was serious about being a member of their protest, that I should take a placard and take part in the ritualistic shouts of "we want change" while scowling at the police. So as not to seem impolite or unsympathetic towards their cause, I took a placard and chanted "we want change". As soon as I finished the chant, the police charged towards us with their riot shields and truncheons, and began to pound the female protestors, dragging them from the crowds and beating them in the bellies with their hard plastic rods. The male protestors turned on me and began booing, accusing me of inciting hatred and violence in their cause, accusing me of provoking the police with the full-throated vehemence of the chant that I had made, although I had not raised my voice above the levels that the menacing bearded men beside me had done, and I felt hard prods in my spine. It occurred to me that I was in danger of being stabbed in the face, so I fought through the crowds of booing protestors and located the pavement, where I walked away from the crowd. I used the placard to deflect the bottles and rocks that were thrown at my retreating frame, and ran towards a cul-de-sac, where I hid for several hours in a shrub. When I emerged, the protest had disbanded. I took my penis in hand as I waited for the bus home.

THE CHARACTER WHO MISSES ANNIKA STRÖMBERG

You come to a state when all is not as circular as things seem. Your radii are less certain. Your circumferii are somewhat loose in the round. You arrive in that place of solid funk. I arrived inside this wonked radii on March the oh-fourth when Madeleine went on tour with reformed Swedish pop act Ace of Base. She had been threatening to walk out on me for months to an intensive tour of upper Sweden. In the 2010s, songwriters Jonas and Ulf had removed the original two female singers (both having committed the cardinal of no longer being twenty and sexy). We had arrived at that stage in our relationship when the louche fortnight of rum, tacos, and fairy lights in a bedroom is no longer viable as a long-term emotional binding, so she went on tour with Ace of Base. Our kissing had started in 2008, when our lips touched following seven hours at the Punctuation Conference. I had pioneered a new punctuation mark and she had applauded with arms aflame. Our kissing lasted seven minutes, a sumo session of lip-on-lip, our two wet lips coming together with the hot intensity of cheese melting on toast. I had eaten melted cheese an hour before, so the literal taste of melted cheese came into our mutual lips atop the figurative one, creating one cheesegasm of a snog. I kissed her on the pavement. Our mutual selves floated upwards in a seven-minute swoon of lip-focused lust, our bodies rooted to the concrete, our loins somewhere overhead in a flock of cormorants. At the eighth minute, in a moment of insane improv, she slipped a tongue between the burning hotness of my lips, introducing her long unfurling seeker around the mucal interzone of my inner mouth, braising the molars at moments. I have to confess, the intake of a kiss is something comparable to the hot upshoot of an idea into one's mental PowerPoint. Later, I lost her to Ulf. Now, I wander around parks recalling our days looking at frenziedly feeding fowl. I miss seeing a swan in the distance, sailing with a litter of grey-furred cygnets in tow, and the anticipation at moving nearer to the swan, the knowledge that looking upon a swan for as long as the swan will tolerate you is coming, and then arriving at the swan, and staring at the swan as her ludicrously svelte neck-cum-head arches with painful certitude towards the water to lap at algae, and the incredulity that these graceful, but utterly fucking sluggish and useless birds, have somehow survived thousands of years without extinction from ravenous swooping vultures. I miss swans. I miss my lover's kisses. I also miss our eating. I miss shoving a fork in a huge plate of mashed potato. Really forking up the mash. Skinning the creamy head from that buttery mound, compacting the mash into separate forts, one side the Sunis, one the Catholics, and staging a cross-theological fracas with the beans, or flooding the mash in a monsoon of gravy, or impressing ridges into the creamy ramparts with the upside of a fork. I miss mash. I miss my lover's kisses.

THE FIRED TV INNOVATOR CHARACTER

The executives sat around a retractable oak-panelled table in their think-space to ponder on the plummeting viewing figures in their factual programmes. "I have noticed that the young people like to watch hardcore pornographic images on their tablets and ipods," I uttered. "I posit that we should include subliminal slides of hardcore pornography in our programmes. For example, in our recent series on the history of the Rwandan people, in between the archival footage of the 1994 Hutu massacre, we might show a couple having full penetrative in a room for about two seconds. These little flashes should appear every thirty seconds or so, spurring people on to watch the rest of the programme, bringing the mutual benefit of mild sexual arousal and historical education." My fellow executives concurred that this was a wonderful idea. The first broadcast of *The Rwandans: A History* was broadcast at 7PM. The reviews for the series were positive, with people praising the depth of archival research and the production values, as well as the thickness of the featured wangs. The decision was made to roll out these short pornographic snippets to other factual programmes of that season. In *The Gnostics: A History*, scenes of fellatio and cunnilingus were incorporated. In *The Origin of the Blues*, full anal penetration was introduced. Five stars across the board. I received a pay rise.

THE CHARACTER PLEASURED BY ELENA BELLAK

Her supple, tequila-tinged tongue tingled the skin on my erect shaft, teasing the tip with a swirl of blissful licks, taking me to heaven as she raised her brown limpid eyes to mine—a perverse, beautiful benediction. Daughter of the village priest, Elena Bellak was a supremely unsaintly bundle of limbs who bucked the trend of the usual provincial slits, unwilling to turn their churchly bodies into instruments of limitless obscenity for legions of oversexed young men—men eager to sluice several centuries of sexual repression into a wondrous flume of semen, flowing endlessly into the ravenous, twitching quims of an endless supply of nun-lashed girls from the convents. Her tongue moving down to the sinewy skin at the base of my cock, she took my balls in her mouth and kept them in the warm bath of her saliva, her little licker attending to each testis in turn. Then she returned to business of sucking, my cock pulsing hard between her sweet lips as I moaned with an abundance of pleasure. Stopping for breath, she observed a strange phenomenon among the beads of semen at the tip. She ran across the room, her plump little bottom wobbling as she located my microscope. Peering closer at my semen, she observed each of them wearing the cassock and mitre of a Catholic bishop. The sight of these ecclesiastically clad come-bubbles made her squirm and squeal, evoking daddy's lashings as she suddenly became repulsed by her own body, her own nakedness, her own casual depravity. She ran towards her clothes at the same ferocity with which she abandoned them. I never heard from her again.

THE HEROIC HANIF KURESHI CHARACTER

On the 5th March 2099, three weeks before the ozonosphere suffocates the entire human race, citizens in the picturesque hamlet Buffock, East

Woking awake to a revolving UFO Pie—fourteen hectares in diameter and nineteen hectares in width—coming to land in meaty resplendence atop the Buffock Hills. The pie, constructed from an impenetrable puff pastry from the Planet Ginsters (constructed as a marketing campaign in 2089) comes to rest on the main hill and looms over the hamlet, blocking out the sun and casting a shadow over Surrey. From its vulvate centre, reinforced with a tungsten 'meat' cover, a shutter opens and begins cannoning the townsfolk.

People flee their homes as flaming pies come blasting through their windows, igniting their front rooms, wounding their children and terrorising the vegetarians. These pie mortars, some of which are shaped more like dough balls, explode upon impact, splatting acidic pork meat from their floury cores, blinding and intoxicating millions with its noxious pig rind extracts. In a bakery, two miles out of town, pie expert Gary Loomis takes a phone call from the Prime Minister. It turns out that he is the only man who can save the nation from total pie annihilation through his unparalleled knowledge of every man who ever baked and how to devour a pie in under two bites.

Choppered into Buffock over the cover of darkness, Gary leaps onto the pie, where he slips on the pastry, falls into the centre and burns up like a meteorite in the sun. The pie takes off and advances toward Shropshire. At this point, there is only one thing for it—the biggest mouth in the planet is called in to cool the surface.

At dusk, I (that is, the writer Hanif Kureishi) blast myself into the sky and suction my way across the pie face, locating that vulvate opening and blowing a whole bellyful of hot air into the centre. The pie swoops through the purple night sky, sending me flying into Suffolk Arts Centre. Crashing into the Pennines, the pie explodes over the north of England, killing 34,000 people. Two weeks later, a day before the human race is obliterated through mass asphyxiation, the world unites in their respect for me, and I am awarded the keys to America, Russia and Palau.

"You're our saviour, Hanif," the world screams.

Yes, I am.

That I am.

THE LAVATORIAL REVENGE CHARACTER

My fortieth birthday party had been an inconclusive combination of ivory candelabra, Swiss chronometers, and oddly stitched trews. Present were friends old and new, lovers old and uninvited, and business associates eyeing me with viperous eyes. I had constructed a hugely successful business manufacturing lavatorial delicacies for the uptight bourgeois who no longer had the means to employ staff to handle the shit from their bowls. My invention was a battery-powered mechanical brush allowing the deployer to electronically unsmear their outgoings while affecting a nonchalant stance over the toilet, pondering perhaps the ormolu clock on the wall opposite until the deed was complete and the chain was ready for flushing. The invention was essentially a mechanised mop, with a small motor pushing the brush bristles in circular whirring motions around the enamel while the user held on to a rubber handle to keep the thing steady. Afterwards, the device could be placed inside a discreet white holder with an engraved slide door, concealed from the lavatorially unobservant as a form of supplementary cistern.

Taking place in the palatial surroundings of Gerwig Hotel in Budapest, I stood atop the balcony of the suite in the manner of Jay Gatsby surveying the festival of parasites below. There was Orbeg Gluteous, my second-in-command, a man supremely reliable at skimming pennies from the accounts whenever my back was turned. I addressed the crowd. "My friends, my fiends, my scrumptious lovers. Today I have become a millionaire. It is an honour to stand here before you. Thank you for all your hard work." I then pulled a large chain concealed below strings of ivy. From above, twelve hectares of lavatorial contents, starring shit, piss, blood, and miscellaneous watery fluids, flooded onto the heads of the assembled. I had always wanted to do that.

THE CHARACTER OF CYNICICYSISTICALDEBOOGIENESS

I coined a series of terms over several years, rolling my terms into one super neologism that became Oxford Dictionary's Word of the Year. Here:

Cynici (2008): A tramp who lurches through the park beating his radioactive meat against a lamppost. He empties the last few drops of alcopops onto his tongue and rates how wretched he feels in metres. Later, he will run around the park squawking at ducks then hurl himself into the pond.

Cysistical (2012): A tendency among doctors to diagnose terminal cysts on patients with a record of perfect health. Usually, the doctors let their patients sweat for two or three months before admitting their 'error' and discharging the patient with a clean bill of health. They are mostly unpleasant people.

Deboogie (2016): To deprogram 1970s disco fanatics by introducing them to a range of music, from soul to reggae to progressive rock. The technique also involves locking the afflicted in a room and pumping in the entire recorded works of The The. Either they lapse into a deep state of shock and remain lost in music, or make a swift comeback.

Cynicicysisticaldeboogieness (2022): A condition among schizophrenics who believe themselves to be tramps with radioactive cocks, doctors with a tendency to diagnose patients with terminal cysts, and 1970s disco fanatics attempting to deprogram themselves with The The records. Very rare in medical circles: only one case in recorded history.

THE CHARACTER WHO NEVER MET ESTZI KEREKES

Whitsuntide was wilting within the sinuous waves of wailing that came from Eszti Kerekes's newborn, Farkas. Following a rowdy bezique tournament where the winner's prize was to kiss and canoodle the women, Eszti found herself part of an orgy in the backroom as the prize was spread evenly among the players. A beery mass of writhing bodies consumed the night—a long, riotous night where randy sailors licked Szalon Sor from the buttocks of blootered, chuckling strumpets, where young virgins suckled the nipples of buxom older women, where soldiers on leave ripped from the frocks from skinny young bodies, bent them over beer casks and thrust their rock-hard cocks in and out their quivering yonis. Desperate for a moment's respite from the screaming child, Eszti bundled her sprog in a shawl and stepped outside, located a medium-sized dumpster in which to temporarily store the unhappy Farkas. She placed him securely on a bed of rubbish bags and closed the lid. All she wanted was an hour of peace, an hour to remember something she had planned to achieve across her itinerant life, to celebrate Whitsuntide free from ear-bleeding cries. She fell asleep instantly and the next morning her child was swallowed up by a refuse lorry. At the rubbish dump, a worker heard muffled screams and retrieved Farkas from the bags, upset but miraculously scratchless. Having no family of his own, the worker raised Farkas himself in accordance with own religious convictions, and the child forged a successful career as a campaigner in an anti-abortion pressure group. After losing Farkas, Eszti was pregnant a year later with a similar baby. I never met her.

THE SNOW JUSTICE CHARACTER

I opened the blinds on the day of my arraignment to an Alaskan neverland of snow. Around me, persons barricaded in their homes squinted dumbly from their windows, lock-jawed commuters exhumed cars from their ice graves, and prancing adolescents sank into punnets of quick-snow to meet their frosty ends.

I walked over to the kettle intending to boil up a brew. My electricity was out, but I had no need to despair. Although the power cut might ruin my perishables, today I had an excuse to avoid being sent to prison.

The previous month, I was caught scalping a small woodland pixie named Jess Sartre by the vending machines at work. Unsure whether it was proper conduct under Section 7, Article 2 of the vending machine preservation act, co-worker Philomena Ricebottom reported me to my boss.

My boss canned me following a fractious meeting where the four general managers agreed by unanimous vote of 4-0 that employees who scalp woodland pixies during office hours have no place in their organisation.

So, helping myself to a bagel, I put on four fur coats and necked a tumbler of soya milk.

No courts.

No judgements.

Snow justice.

THE CHARACTER FROM TISZASAS

At the end of the war, holed up in the village of Tiszasas with two Nazis, I was forced at gunpoint to play a game of hangman. Usually, this game takes place on a piece of paper. This time, the game involved me guessing the name of a man stood on the gallows with a rope around his neck. I had six wrong guesses, one for the head, torso, legs, and arms. I guessed Z, Y, G, E, C, and S, then the man struggled against the rope until the struggling stopped. The man's name was Alan Wilmott, he was a British soldier. I felt relieved. No one in Hungary has ever shed a tear for a dead British soldier.

THE CHARACTER OF BREATHTAKING WISDOM

You should never put a live rat inside a freezer. I arrived home to a frozen rat, twitching in its throes atop my steaks. There is nothing to be gained from placing a live rat into someone's freezer. The rat will contaminate the meat and startle anyone who opens the freezer. If the person who placed this rat in my freezer were here, I would tell them: 'My friend, there is nothing to be gained from placing a live rat in someone's freezer.' And there isn't. There really isn't.

AND SO ON

AD INFINITUM

M.J. Nicholls is the author of *Condemned to Cymru*, *Trimming England*, *Scotland Before the Bomb*, *The 1002nd Book to Read Before You Die*, *The House of Writers*, *The Quiddity of Delusion*, and *A Postmodern Belch*. He lives in Glasgow.